MURDER ON THE MOUNTAIN

M.J. Rossi

MURDER ON THE MOUNTAIN

M.J. Rossi

HUDSON HOUSE

FIRST EDITION
ISBN 978-1-58776-958-0
Library of Congress catalog card number: 2014939774

Manufactured in the United States of America
NetPublications, Inc
675 Dutchess Turnpike, Poughkeepsie, NY 12603
www.hudsonhousepub.com (800) 724-1100

HUDSON HOUSE

675 Dutchess Turnpike, Poughkeepsie, NY 12603
www.hudsonhousepub.com (800) 724-1100

DEDICATION TO:

"Maryann.... My Wife.... My Best Friend....My Rock."

"We learn more in our valley experiences than on our mountaintops."

FOREWORD

Many people enjoy reading mysteries. So often we encounter baffling circumstances in our lives. We, as humans, always look to solve whatever does not make sense. But as we do this we also want to find peace.

As you read this novel some parts may seem real whereas others may seem surreal. Also each chapter has a High Peaks highlight. If you have ever visited the Adirondacks maybe you have enjoyed one of these hiking adventures. Perhaps you reside in the area and you are familiar with the beautiful sights, particularly some of the spectacular views.

I hope you enjoy this journey.

PROLOGUE

PRESENT DAY

The snow had been coming down heavy for the past few hours. The High Peaks are absolutely stunning no matter what time of the year. The fall has always been a favorite time for both residents and visitors as the colors of the tree foliage are quite magnificent. The winter though could bring about all different types of adventures.

In fact, the regular visitor to the mountain ranges could always find some new place to explore. Vacationers have always descended upon this region as so many grand hotels had sprung up throughout the Adirondacks. In the late 1800's tubercular patients used the region as a mecca due to the crisp and fresh air.

There are numerous historical attractions along with a tremendous amount of hiking trails for any age. The New York State legislature in 1892 created the Adirondack State Park consisting of Adirondack Forest Preserve land plus all privately owned land within a somewhat arbitrary boundary. The Adirondack State Park is the largest park in the United States outside of Alaska.

The town of Keene was at a strategic location with the intersection of Route 9N and Route 73 bringing thousands of people through the area on a daily basis. During the nineteenth century Keene was ringed by railroads. But by the twentieth century people in the area experienced the demise of the railroads. The automobile allowed people to become mobile.

No matter where you may venture in the Adirondacks there is something to explore. It would not matter what time of the year it might be, a person could discover something. There was always something going on. A person could easily get lost with some adventure. Sometimes the situation could suddenly become difficult. It could be because a person felt invincible. Or the individual had underestimated a situation. Maybe the person was manipulated. Perhaps poor judgment was utilized.

That is exactly what happened to Sean Metcalf during this particular winter. It was a winter like no other for Sean. He was young and naïve. Perhaps he was somewhat of a believer that all people could be trustworthy. His dad always taught him to see the good in any person he encountered. He had done just that even though some skepticism began to emerge. But that happens to all of us as we get older and we have seen more of what life offers us.

Sometimes life throws curves at us and we have to prepare ourselves for them. But sometimes we are unable to see a situation arise until it has gripped us and possibly consume us. No matter what a person needs to keep an optimistic attitude. Never give up hope.

Sean was in for an adventure though. He would be tested. His faith in others would be questioned. He would wonder what was happening around him. He would seek refuge with things and people he believed he could count on.

Life provides many trials and tribulations. Sean was about to face these. How he could do so would be tested. So many people say we become stronger through the many trials and hardships we endure in life.

PART ONE

"Hope is the anchor of our soul."

CHAPTER ONE

THE NAME "HIGH PEAKS" WAS GIVEN TO THE 46 ADIRONDACK MOUNTAINS THAT WERE HIGHER THAN 4000 FEET…

"I told you, there is no one at the cabin."

Detective Metcalf would not listen to what the gray haired lady told him. Ryan Metcalf had been living at the base of the small hamlet of Keene, surrounded by the High Peaks, since he was a child. It has always been a popular place as a starting point for hikers to ascend Mt. Marcy, the highest mountain in New York State, along with other destinations.

Ryan's parents had left the Canadian urban area and relocated to Keene in upstate New York when Ryan was four years old. And now forty-eight years later he was about to come upon a mysterious situation. Mrs. Anna Hamilton had known Detective Ryan Metcalf for the past forty-eight years. Even though it may not seem so to an acquaintance, Anna and Ryan greatly respected one another. Their families grew up together. They were each aware of one another's trials and tribulations even though they rarely spoke about their personal lives.

Again she said, "There is no one at the cabin!"

Metcalf nodded at Hamilton but did not say anything. She looked quite aged. There were deep wrinkles around her eyes; distinct cat's cradles were evident. The same was true at the corners of her lips. She was only four years older than Metcalf but anyone would not guess that to be so. Even though she was neatly dressed she was not a stunning woman.

Anna had been married twice and widowed twice as well. Anna Hamilton's first husband, Sid Messier, died two years after they were married. His death left Anna as a young widow with a little girl to take care of. Anna was deeply in love with Sid. She could not imagine at the time how she could live without him.

Sid's boat had been found at a nearby pond with all of his fishing equipment tucked neatly in the rowboat.Sid was a very detailed oriented individual. In fact, he was quite predictable. Anna knew exactly what he would prepare for his lunch. He always took a roast beef sandwich, two apples and a small bag of walnuts with him whenever journeying to the pond. He also would always return at exactly six o'clock to have his supper. So Anna was quite anxious when Sid had not returned from his fishing outing.

Sid had frequented the pond by Marcy Dam on a regular basis. The Trail Ranger knew Sid by name. It was a very warm August day. It was more humid than normal for the Adirondack region, especially since it had been a very wet month of August. Usually there are three to four inches of precipitation per month but not that August.

His body was found six weeks later; well, what was left of his decomposed body. It was found in the nearby woods by Marcy Dam. It was odd no one had immediately discovered Sid's body. But when a hiker did so, the eyes and soft parts of the body were gone, as animals had apparently found his remains. An array of wildlife inhabited the forest whether it was raccoons, often carrying rabies, coyotes, fox, deer, bobcats or bears. So animals had mauled Sid's body.

A bullet wound was in the back of Sid's skull. His murderer was not apprehended, though Mrs. Hamilton believed it was a suicide. An autopsy was not performed even though it was recommended by the county coroner.The coroner did say he could overrule Anna's request as he could declare Sid's death as a mysterious death. Anna had insisted that she did not want Sid's body more mutilated than what he had already had been. The coroner respected her request. Anna though seemed somewhat mysterious about not having an autopsy completed. Why wouldn't a bullet hole in the back of Sid's skull alarm her?

The amazing part was that the funeral director was able to piece Sid's body into a presentable state for Sid's wake.

The county coroner was concerned that an autopsy would not be performed. The coroner knew not to press matters as the death of Sid was not declared to be suspicious. The coroner asked the district attorney to pursue the matter but that did not occur as the district attorney said he had more prominent cases to deal with.

Anna was absolutely devastated by Sid's death. Anna was left alone to raise their little daughter. The people of Keene were so wonderful to her and her daughter. She had contemplated leaving the area but changed her mind as she experienced the unbelievable outpouring of goodwill by so many friends and strangers.

CHAPTER TWO

IT WAS LATER DETERMINED THAT ONE HIGH PEAK WAS OVERLOOKED AND FOUR OF THE ORIGINAL GROUP WERE ACTUALLY A LITTLE LOWER…

Detective Metcalf again asked for a third time about the cabin and its potential occupants.

Mrs. Hamilton expressed, “No one is there. But, fine, I will take you up the trail road. Let me get the keys to the cabin.”

She walked into the kitchen and retrieved the set of keys, placed a log into the wood burning stove and placed a pair of gloves into her coat pocket. She wrapped her scarf around her neck and mouth rather snuggly. The cold air could cause her to start to cough and lose her breath. Anna had been a long time asthma sufferer since she was a teenager. Twice she had almost lost her life as the asthma attacks had been rather severe. She had discovered that sometimes stress or a sudden change in the weather could bring on an episode.The snow was picking up speed. The region was preparing for a major storm to blow in overnight.

As Metcalf waited outside Anna Hamilton’s house, he could not avoid noticing two framed photographs on the windowsill of Anna’s living room. They seemed to be pictures of her deceased husbands as she posed in both of them. It was known about town by the long time residents that Anna’s second husband had drowned a few months ago as he was out looking for their sixteen-year-old daughter. His body was found two days after he left the house to look for Sabrina. His body was rather swollen. Anna identified his body at the county morgue. She did not want a public viewing as she felt Matthew’s body did not resemble what he looked like before he died. Again, she baffled the authorities by not having an autopsy performed.

People of Keene knew Matthew Hamilton well. He descended from the Paine family, as Benjamin Paine was a famous early citizen of Keene. Matthew’s family also was previously employedand ran the Keene Center House. It was frequented by many travelers and later became known as the Owl's Head House.

Nearby is the Owl's Head Mountain trail frequented by many hikers. It is a pretty easy 1.1 mileround trip hike. People of the area often commented on the outstanding view at the summit of the mountain. When the Keene Center was in business, Matthew's father would often escort hikers on the Owl's Head Mountain trail. He was rather endowed with the history of the region.

Matthew Hamilton went looking for Sabrina upon her fleeing the house when she learned her mother had lost her teaching position at the local school. Anna had been a mathematics teacher and due to last minute budget shortfalls her position was eliminated. The townspeople were heartbroken for Anna; and for Sabrina too, as Anna had become a two-time widow. She was also an outstanding educator.

No one, at the time, suspected any type of foul play with the deaths of Sid Messier and Matthew Hamilton. But how could such odd circumstances occur to two of Anna's husbands. Why did she insist on not having an autopsy completed of Sid's body?Or of Matthew Hamilton as well?

Ryan Metcalf was always intrigued by mysterious situations. As an investigator he was trained to pick up upon any type of minute detail that could solve a case. Over the years, he, himself, had been called by various police agencies to assist with their respective investigations. The deaths of both of Anna Hamilton's husbands found him wondering to the validity of the findings. Anna seemed very reluctant to delve into the details of her personal life. It made her somewhat melancholy whenever she did so.

CHAPTER THREE

ALL BUT FOUR OF THE HIGH PEAKS ARE LOCATED IN THE KEENE-KEENE VALLEY-LAKE PLACID AREA…

The snow was coming down quite heavily. The state and county highway departments have numerous fleets of snowplows toiling night and day to keep the roads free of snow and ice. Some of the highway workers had been commenting as to how brutal this particular winter season had become. They were having some difficulty as to where to place all of the accumulating snow. But the Adirondack roads, after a deep snow, are in better condition than many suburban roads after a modest flurry.

People went about their business. Some stopped and talked to their friends and shop owners as if it was a warm summer day. So no one in Keene seemed to be fazed by the intensity of the snowfall. It was a rarity if any of the shops and stores ever closed due to a snowstorm. Businesses usually made a profit during any type of storm, unless the conditions were deemed dangerous.

Anna finally emerged from her house with the keys to the cabin. She climbed into Detective Metcalf's SUV. The inside of the vehicle was surprisingly clean and rather cozy. She was rather surprised that the vehicle was not littered with fast food wrappers, newspapers and other items. It had a warm feel to it, especially with the chilly weather. This made Anna feel more comfortable.

They began the ride up the mountain trail to the cabin. The roads were becoming slick but a "bare roads" policy was in effect for the North Country. Sand and salt had been applied liberally but not necessarily on the back roads leading to the cabins located in obscure parts of the woods. Most of the upper roads or paths were not paved. They were predominantly graveled surfaces maintained by the homeowners. Most of those people had their own pickup trucks with snow plows attached to them. The surfaces were cold due to the temperatures being in the low twenties during the day.

Metcalf asked Anna, "Why do you seem so reluctant to go to the cabin?"

"I'm not."

"Well, I am sorry I bothered you to go up to the cabin."

"You didn't."

She did not seem that interested in engaging in a conversation. There was some silence between them as the visibility ahead was quite limited. Anna took off her gloves and hat as she began to feel warm inside the detective's vehicle. Her gray hair was pulled back in a ponytail. Her cheeks were reddened and she was not wearing any make-up.

Metcalf tried to re-engage Anna in a conversation.

"I saw those pictures on your windowsill." He hesitated. He did not want her to be distracted or get upset. She did not seem to be so.

"Oh. They are my husbands. They both died. I thought you knew that."

"I'm sorry. I did know but I was curious as to the circumstances of their deaths. I hope you do not mind me asking."

"Don't be sorry. I do not mind talking to you about them." This was out of character for Anna as she rarely spoke of her personal life with anyone.

The trail road took a quick incline. Even though the snow was coming down hard, it was not difficult for Metcalf to follow the trail road as it was well maintained. The town maintenance crews had an excellent reputation of keeping up with the conditions of the back roads and trails throughout the year.

But before she could discuss the circumstances of her husbands' deaths, Anna pointed ahead and said, "There is the cabin."

Metcalf looked ahead and could also see the cabin through the lit up large snowflakes. He seemed disappointed that he did not get to listen to Anna's explanation of the deaths of her two husbands. He knew both deaths were of a mysterious nature, but he never suspected Anna of any misdeeds. Anna Hamilton was never suspected by the authorities of any wrongdoing. And there was no good reason for her to be a suspect. She was deeply in love with her first husband and she would have no good reason whatsoever to murder her second husband.

Anna was a longtime resident of Keene. She had been elected as a village trustee for ten years in a row. She also served as a library board trustee as well. She became interested in that position as she was a frequent visitor of the Keene Library. Her reputation was stellar. People looked to her for both her wisdom and real understanding of what it meant to be a resident of the area.

As they came upon the cabin he said, "A light is on."

Anna looked puzzled. She knew she had locked up the cabin a few weeks ago. Perhaps hunters were using the dwelling. She did not particularly like that idea especially since she had shut off the electric power unit at the back of the cabin.She also did not like how the hunters would leave the premises in such disarray.

Anna had just been up to the cabin a few days ago to check on it and to assure that the snow storms had no ill effects on the dwelling. She would always check on the condition of the roof along with the chimney flume. She was proud of the way she would keep the place in good condition.

CHAPTER FOUR

THE TWO HIGHEST PEAKS ARE MARCY AND ALGONQUIN…

Ryan Metcalf slowed his SUV down. Anna seemed somewhat agitated as they approached the cabin. Not only was the cabin lit up but smoke was emerging from the chimney. She opened the passenger door just as Metcalf brought the vehicle to a halt. She approached the front door of the cabin. There were lights inside illuminating the first floor living room area. She had the cabin keys in her right hand but instead decided to knock. Footsteps could be heard from the inside of the cabin approaching the front door. Quickly the door opened. Detective Metcalf gasped, which was unusual for him as not much really startled him.

He then said, "What are you doing here?"

"Hello Dad."

The young man looked over at Anna Hamilton and simply said, "Who are you?

"This is Anna Hamilton. You remember her."

Sean's father was concerned that he did not recognize Anna Hamilton even though she had a winter hat on. Sean had known her for quite a few years, in fact, ever since he was born. Sean's father was concerned that Sean seem distracted. He also seemed to be quite disoriented.

Behind the person at the doorway there was a sudden movement by someone. The door opened wider but at first no one was there. Mrs. Hamilton yelled out, "Who is there? What is going on?"

Then a young lady appeared behind the young man. Mrs. Hamilton gasped. There was a great amount of puzzlement across her face. She began to have trouble catching her breath.

"Oh no. It can't be. Sabrina!"

Ryan Metcalf looked confused and looked at both of them. "Sean, why are you here? Why do you look so frightened?"

Sean and Sabrina did not expect to see their respective parents on the front porch of the cabin. Neither one of them knew what to say to either Sean's father or Sabrina's mother. They just stood there.

CHAPTER FIVE

HAYSTACK IS ONE OF THE MOST DEMANDING HIKES DUE TO ITS RUGGED TERRAIN AND HIKING DISTANCE…

The winds were swirling. Anna became lightheaded and grabbed onto a porch post. Detective Metcalf realized Anna might pass out. She held onto his coat. She could not stand up on her own. He walked her into the cabin and sat her down in a chair by the wood-burning stove. The smoke in the room seemed to deter her breathing even more so. Anna sat down and closed her eyes.

The cabin was warm. The fire was roaring in the black potbellied stove. Sabrina unbuttoned her mother's coat and took off her hat as well. Anna's skin felt clammy as she continued to keep her eyes closed. She was not having as much difficulty with her breathing but she seemed lethargic.

Sabrina went into the kitchen, filled the teakettle with water, set out four teacups and returned to the living room. Sabrina sat down next to her mother. She patted Anna's forehead with a cool cloth. Anna opened her eyes but did not utter a word.

Ryan could not believe his son, Sean, had answered the door. He was startled by Sean's physical appearance. He looked like he had lost some weight and he had grown a full beard to compliment his long brown hair. Ryan always knew his son to be vibrant looking and this was not the case at this time. Sean looked exhausted yet he seemed happy to see his father.

The teakettle began to whistle. Sabrina returned to the kitchen to tend to the tea. Anna kept her eyes opened and was looking at detective Metcalf and his son. Ryan and his son had not spoken to one another in the last six months. He thought Sean was up in Canada at his grandparent's house. Ryan's mother lived there alone and had been there for quite a few years after Ryan's father had passed away. And then to discover that Anna's daughter, Sabrina, was at the cabin as well caused him angst.

Sabrina came back into the living room. She had placed the four cups of steeping tea on a tray and placed it on a table by the wood burning stove. Anna sat up in a more erect position and began to fix her own cup of tea. She still had not spoken since coming inside the cabin. Sabrina went back into the kitchen and returned with a plate of chocolate chip cookies.

Ryan turned to his son, Sean, and asked,

"What is going on?"

Anna nodded her head in agreement with Ryan's question. Sean looked over at Sabrina. She blinked her eyes a few times and simply said,

"Go ahead. Tell them. It is time they knew what was going on."

Both Ryan and Anna looked back and forth at their children, not knowing what to expect Sean to tell the two of them.

ANNA HAMILTON

"Life is worth living…no matter what!"

Anna had lived in Keene for most of her life. When she was a little girl she enjoyed swimming in the local streams. She was always the first one to jump into the cool refreshing waters. She particularly liked going to the waterfalls. As she got older she was dared by friends to jump off the cliffs. She only hesitated because she knew her mother would vehemently insist that she not do so. But she took the dare many times and was never harmed.

As she grew older she began to take a great interest in reading. She would frequent the local library and the librarian would always give Anna different suggestions. Anna particularly liked to read mystery stories along with the local history of the Adirondacks region. She always tried to figure out the endings of the mystery novels. But she was more interested in the book if she could not figure out the mystery herself. She always found a good mystery to be one that kept you wondering.

Anna always felt a sense of comfort whenever she read. An aunt of hers once said,

"Reading helps me to escape for a while. It helps me to forget what is going on around me, especially if things are difficult."

Anna took her aunt's words to heart. Many a times she took her aunt's advice. If Anna was not immersed in reading a good book she would write in her journal or scribe short stories. She had quite a creative mind. Anna also took great comfort in keeping every single letter her first husband, Sid, had written to her. Whenever she wanted to be close to him, especially after his sudden death, she would venture into her attic, take out the letters she had placed in a wooden chest, untie the ribbons she had wrapped them in, select a few and sit down and read. She enjoyed reading various ones of interest. A particular one she returned to, read as follows:

Dear Anna,

I loved you the moment I set eyes on you. I had always wanted to meet someone like you but thought it could never happen to me. You have taught me how to truly treat a lady with a great sense of admiration. With a great level of love.And a feeling of mutual respect.

You are my light. You are my inspiration. You are my spirit. I hope I can always reciprocate all you are to me. I want us to grow old together.

Anna would always have to pause and place the letter down for a few moments as Sid's words truly made her sad; she missed him so much. After regaining her composure she could continue.

I know I will always provide for you the best life can offer us. Through prayer I know we will live a long life together. I pray every night that nothing will ever separate us and our love for one another. I will always love and treasure you.

All my love,

Sid

The letters always provided her great sense of comfort. Sid had taken such care with scribing his letters to Anna. He was not a man to express his inner most thoughts out loud. But he truly knew how to express himself in words. His death would always be difficult for her to adjust to; his death was quite a shock. But she knew Sid would not want her to wallow in his death. He would often say. "Living is for the living. Live your life."

Anna's aunt died unexpectedly when Anna was fourteen years old. She felt as if she had lost her best friend. It was the first time she had to deal with the passing of a close family member. She had no one to talk to about it. Anna's mother did not seem to be overly upset by the loss of her sister. At the time, Anna did not really think too much about that. Yet she did wonder if her mother was envious of the relationship Anna had with her mother's sister.

CHAPTER SIX

BIG SLIDE HAS SPECTACULAR VIEWS...

Keene is contained within a 165 square mile area. The cabin inhabited by Sabrina and Sean was in remarkable condition, especially since it had been erected in 1820. Two acres away, up the trail road, another cabin stood. It was also built in 1820. The Hamilton family owned 350 acres of land; Anna had become a very wealthy woman after the death of her two husbands. When she first married Sid, her first husband, he made her aware that he owned a good amount of land in the area.

Anna did not realize the extent of Matthew's wealth until he passed away.Between Sid's wise investments and Matthew's family wealth, Anna was well to do. She knew she did not have to ever concern herself again with money matters. She hired a local accountant to monitor her estate. He was recommended to her by a prominent local attorney, Sydney Emerson.

Anna Hamilton was familiar with the cabin she was seated in. It was built in sturdy fashion. The first floor has a large living room area with a side room and a kitchen along with a small bathroom. A rather large window in the main room looks upon a picturesque view of the High Peaks. Recently the area outside the cabin had been excavated by a local construction company. Theworkers had enhanced the spectacular view. Twenty-two of the forty-six High Peaks were visible from this vantage point. Anyone familiar with the region would be in awe of the view. Throughout the area, a person could come in contact with rather prominent scenic views. This one was breath taking.

The High Peaks region derives its name by the fact that it contains all of the Adirondacks peaks with elevations over four thousand feet as well as numerous other mountains under that elevation. Hundreds of avid hikers have climbed all forty six of the high peaks. Anna was one of those individuals. She had hiked the highest peak in New York State, Mount Marcy, on ten different occasions. Her latest journey took place a few weeks after Matthew Hamilton's death. She hiked the trail by herself as a soul searching expedition more than anything else. Sabrina was worried about her mother hiking by herself but she knew it was something her mother needed to do.

Anna was having difficulty breathing but she was accustomed to the high altitudes of the region. Sabrina was quite concerned as Ryan went about checking Anna's vitals. Sean noticed the snow was coming down at a heavy pace.

Suddenly the electricity shut off. Fortunately the roaring fire had warmed up the cabin. Even the upstairs was nice and warm. There are three bedrooms on the upper floor. The wood burning stove had been recently replaced by Anna herself. She had always been rather handy. She was able to rebuild one of the upstairs bedrooms to accommodate the larger beds she had constructed.

Things became rather quiet between all of them. Ryan and Anna patiently waited for either Sean or Sabrina to speak and inform them of their situation. Ryan was used to Sean's long silences as this was his pattern of behavior whenever a difficult moment occurred. When he was younger, particularly when he had done something wrong or knew of information about a particular situation, he became rather quiet. Ryan thought of it as being stubborn and pigheaded. But Ryan realized this was not a simple episode. Sabrina, too, had not really looked at her mother to give any type of an explanation.

CHAPTER SEVEN

CASCADE'S 360 DEGREE VIEWS AT THE SUMMIT BRING LOTS OF VISITORS…

Sean's dad was becoming impatient; this was not a common characteristic that Ryan would normally exhibit. Ryan was always patient; this was a distinct quality he was known for especially when he was investigating a case. His fortitude usually enabled him to break even the most difficult cases he encountered.

Ryan finally asked his son, Sean, "When did you get here?"

Sean hesitated but then responded,

"Two days ago."

"And Sabrina?"

"She's been here for two weeks but she wasn't ready to see her mother."

Anna was feeling better as she sipped her tea. Her daughter, Sabrina, kept her distance on the other side of the living room. The winds were howling outside. The snow was coming down heavier than usual that even Ryan was getting worried by the severity of the storm. The gusts were causing the snow to drift up onto the front porch. The snow was coming down so heavy that Sabrina was lighting candles, as she figured the electricity would probably be out for some time.

The snowstorm seemed to be worsening as minutes went by. Each of them realized they would probably be spending the night at the cabin. This would be a concern for Sean's father as he had business to tend to back at his house. He had promised a close friend he would give his professional and expert opinion on a case his friend was dealing with in upstate New York. But he knew he had no choice but to put that on the back burner.

Anna did not seem as though she could travel yet. Her face was rather pale and she was shivering. Sabrina looked over to Sean and his father.

"I do not understand what is going on," stated Ryan.

He had taken off his dark blue parka, gloves and hat. He then proceeded to sit down on the couch. Sean hesitated to respond. Finally he spoke up.

"You will be able to understand if you have patience." He then walked over to Sabrina as he probably realized his answer was rather abrupt. As he stood by Sabrina he whispered something into her ear.

Ryan was becoming rather agitated. Anna just looked at Sabrina. She, as well, was confused by the situation. Neither Sabrina nor Sean seemed ready to give an explanation.

Ryan got up from his seat and walked over to the window to look out at the hard falling snow. The view from the window looked out at Hurricane Mountain. Even though this mountain was not one of the infamous forty sixers, it was a rather frequented trail for hikers. The vertical face near Hurricane Mountain's incredible view at the summit contains a weathered *1776* chiseled into the rock. Some local people have insisted the carving was done by American soldiers on watch that year as they kept track of the British contingent as a follow up to the recently rebel captured Fort Ticonderoga. Hurricane Mountain could provide on a clear day views from Lake Champlain to the East Branch of the Ausable River.

But this was not on Ryan Metcalf's mind. Usually the view of Hurricane Mountain would normally provide him with serenity. That was not the case now. He began to turn around and say something but opted not to. Sean realized his father was keeping his temper in check.

PART TWO

CHAPTER EIGHT

FORTY-EIGHT YEARS EARLIER

GOTHICS IS ONE OF THE GREATEST PEAKS IN THE NORTHEAST…

Ryan Metcalf was just four years old. His parents, older brother and sister, and Ryan had just moved from southeastern Canada to Keene, New York. The hamlet of Keene is approximately fifteen miles outside of Lake Placid, home of the 1932 and 1980 Winter Olympics. Keene was, and still is, a rural Adirondacks community. Families worked at the sawmills and grist mills during the nineteenth century and early twentieth century. Many families, such as the Hulls, the Holts and the Nortons, have resided in the Keene area for generations.

The Metcalf family's arrival was quite an event as Reverend Metcalf was appointed the new minister of the Regional Protestant Church. The people were excited to see such a young man to lead their congregation. But one year later, to the day, Reverend Metcalf went missing. Even though Ryan was only five years old, he was devastated by the situation. He realized his Dad would never be seen again. His brother, Michael, assumed the role of surrogate father. Michael was only eleven years old when their father mysteriously vanished. Their father was a genuine family oriented man. Yet, why did he suddenly disappear? Did he take flight? Was he murdered?

The people of Keene spent six days and nights scouring the area. Even many of the hiking trails were searched. Fortunately, it was the month of July when Reverend Metcalf disappeared and not during the brutal wintertime. The black flies were still out in force. This was extremely unusual as the month of June was the particular time the black flies were notorious for causing havoc in the Adirondacks. But this did not deter the many people from continuing the harrowing search.

After six days the search was halted. The Reverend's wife was very appreciative of the people's efforts. A memorial service was held three months later, during the Columbus Day Weekend. One of the longtime Keene residents, Jane

Henery, gave a very solemn eulogy at the packed church. Jane knew the Metcalfs before they arrived from Canada. She was a widow with a young daughter, named Anna. Anna was a beautiful girl who would light up a room.

Jane's words were well thought out and elegantly stated. "Even though Reverend Metcalf was only a part of our community for a year he touched our lives in such great ways."

She paused for a few moments and then continued, "Let me ask all of you a few questions. First, how many of you knew Reverend Metcalf?" Every hand went up in the air. Many looked around at the gatherers.

"And how many of you ever received a note or a card from Reverend Metcalf to help lift your spirits or to simply express his appreciation?" Practically every person put a hand up.

"And I'm sure many of us have had a conversation with Reverend Metcalf and he made you feel like you was the only and most important person in the world." So many heads nodded. A number of congregants began to cry. Jane concluded by saying, "Remember he left us in better shape than what we were before he arrived. We miss him so much."

The assistant reverend completed the service with a prayer of thanksgiving and blessed everyone. The congregation departed the church in a very slow manner. It was as if they did not want to depart. Reverend Metcalf's spirit was within each of them. But there was also some gossiping occurring as to what happened to Reverend Metcalf. Some thought it was somewhat odd that a memorial service was held but a body was never discovered.

CHAPTER NINE

STREET MOUNTAIN IS OFTEN CLIMBED WITH NYE MOUNTAIN...

Keene is abundant with hiking trails. The Adirondack Park has more than two thousand miles of marked hiking trails that lead to ponds, waterfalls, peaks, ice caves and gorges. After the memorial service a group of mourners and the Metcalf family made their way to the Cascade trail to pay final respects for Reverend Metcalf by placing an American flag at the foot of the path.

Cascade seemed like the natural place to have a memorial for Reverend Metcalf. During his short time in Keene, he had climbed this frequented trail three times. Reverend Metcalf often told the story of the first recorded ascent of Cascade that occurred in 1872. A local, Lon Pierce, set a trap for a bear on the summit of the mountain. His trapping endeavor was a success. The reverend often shared this story to encourage people to never give up on something they wanted to achieve.

Ryan looked at it as if it made no sense to its importance or reason. As a five year old he wondered what happened to his father and why he was not with them. He could not figure out why they all acted like his father was dead. He often wondered why his mother did not inquire more so than she did. As the years went by this thought seemed to consume Ryan. Whenever Ryan asked his brother Michael about their father's disappearance, he did not really give any type of an adequate response.

But Ryan, even though he was only five years old, could hear some of the people at the memorial service wondering what really happened to his father. He heard one old timer speculate that the reverend ran off with a mistress. Another longtime resident thought the reverend may have returned to Canada. A couple of people speculated that Reverend Metcalf wanted to blend into the wilderness and seek adventures similar to Lon Pierce.

They departed the Cascade trail and the Metcalf family went back to the cabin on the mountain to return to their changed lives. Even though it had only been three months since Reverend Metcalf disappeared it seemed like a lifetime. Ryan had a very difficult time with not having his father around to parent and guide him. It was such an enormous void. Reverend Metcalf never was to be seen alive by his family or the residents of Keene again.

CHAPTER TEN

THE PRESENT

PORTER MOUNTAIN IS OFTEN CLIMBED WITH CASCADE MOUNTAIN AND IS USUALLY LESS CROWDED...

Sabrina collapsed to the floor. Sean immediately tended to her. Anna Hamilton was crying and at the same time screamed for Ryan to call for assistance. There was also the concern of the ferocious snowstorm occurring. The wind was gusting at over forty miles per hour. Sabrina's face was ashen colored and blood was evident on her lower extremities.

Ryan yelled out, "Where is the phone?" He looked around frantically, which was also very uncharacteristic for him. Ryan had always been known to keep an even demeanor, especially when turmoil occurred.

"My cell phone does not work at this altitude."

Sean pointed in the direction of the kitchen. Ryan ran over to the phone. Anna looked confused and bewildered. She then said, "What is wrong with Sabrina?"

Sean hesitated to respond. But then after a few moments he quietly said, "She is pregnant."

"What? By who? You?"

There was a long silence. All that could be heard was the wind. Sean's father returned to the living room.

Sean finally said, "I do not know. She asked me to meet her here to tell me."

Ryan looked over to Sabrina and then said to Sean and Anna, "The telephone works. An EMS vehicle is on the way. Hopefully they can make their way up the trail road." Ryan then went over to his son and asked, "Sean, please tell me what is happening. When did you really arrive here?"

Sean looked up at his father and said, "Last night."

Sean looked away from his father and back over at Sabrina. In a low voice he said, "I did not want you or Mom to know I was here and I do not really want to talk to you now."

Ryan looked at his son in amazement. He did not know what was going on. This was very unlike Sean to act in this manner. Ryan knew there was more to the situation besides Sabrina being pregnant. Up until six months ago, Sean and he were on good terms.

The headlights of the EMS vehicle could be seen through the living room window. The snowfall had seemed to slow down even though a good number of inches had accumulated. Ryan went to the cabin door and opened it to greet the two emergency workers. He knew both of them.

RYAN METCALF

"Live the life you love. Love the life you live."

Ryan Metcalf's life became dramatically better upon meeting Rita. He knew after just going on one date with her, he wanted to spend the rest of his life with Rita. Ryan had dealt with so many issues as he grew up. His older brother, Michael, was his protector. Michael went as far as to defend him and Ryan whenever their father would get rather aggravated with them for what seemed to be very little issues of concern.

One time Michael confronted their father over the loss of a bike they had taken into town. Reverend Metcalf's reaction was startling as he slapped Michael across the face. Ryan was horrified. He was unsure of how to react. Why would their father suddenly haul off and hit Michael? Ryan from that time onward became fearful of his father's temper. Amazingly Michael showed no reaction upon been hit by their father.

Ryan's life went into a period of depression as he entered his teen years. Even though his father disappeared when Ryan was only five years old he missed him. Even though his father exhibited rather sporadic angry behaviors at times, he missed him.

Ryan, even at the age of five years old, thought it was odd that no one in his family seemed to shed a tear or even show any type of sadness. He did not know what to say. No one in school or at home talked about his father. It was as if his father never existed.

Ryan had always felt his father was out there somewhere alive. He never felt his father had died. He promised himself he would continue to seek the answers as to his father's mysterious disappearance. Ryan at times would make inquiries with different law enforcement agents he came in contact. Ryan also was cautioned by his wife, Rita, to not let this consume him. Most days he did not do so but every once in a while he researched various leads as some contacts were able to provide Ryan with credible information. A few times throughout the years, Ryan would travel to various locations in Canada hoping to find his father. One trip, in particular, was deemed hopeful as his closest friend, Jason Euling, believed he had spotted reverend Metcalf in a small hamlet outside the Montreal area. But to no avail when Ryan reached the destination, there was no one at the empty cabin.

Ryan did know though that his family was his foundation. Rita was everything he could hope to find in a wife. She was loving, understanding and sensible. He knew he could always count on her steadiness with whatever situation they encountered in their lives.

CHAPTER ELEVEN

ESTHER MOUNTAIN WAS NAMED AFTER ESTHER McCOMB WHO AT THE AGE OF 15 MADE THE FIRST RECORDED ASCENT TO THE PEAK…

Sabrina's baby arrived three days later. The bleeding she experienced had no ill effect on the delivery of the infant. Her labor though went on for over twenty four hours. Sabrina experienced such long contractions that her doctor had become somewhat concerned. But Sabrina was determined to deliver naturally with no pain killers whatsoever. The baby was healthy, weighed eight pounds and two ounces and Sabrina wanted to name him after Sean's father. So the baby was named Ryan Mason. Mason was her mother's father's middle name.

Sabrina urged Sean to contact his father and tell him and Sean's mother what they decided. But Sean was reticent to talk to his father yet. Sabrina was also excited that her mother was back in her life. She decided to stay with Sabrina and the baby so she could help out. Sabrina welcomed this. Sabrina knew her mother would be a great help for her with the care of the baby. Sabrina was so nervous about how to take care of an infant. Sabrina's mom quickly put Sabrina at ease and urged Sabrina to get some much needed rest.

Again Sabrina talked to Sean about seeing his parents.

"Go and see them. They will be excited."

"I can't yet."

"Why not? Do you want me to go with you?"

Sean nodded his head from side to side. Sean still had not told his mother and father yet about the other reason he had disappeared for six months. This would be more difficult than them finding out about Sabrina and the baby.

He left the cabin and made his way down the trail road by using his ATV. It took about ten minutes to get to the Metcalf's house. He knew this would be a very difficult conversation. He did not know how he would begin to inform his parents of the other details. He knew they would always comfort him, regardless of his situation.

CHAPTER TWELVE

ALGONQUIN IS THE SECOND HIGHEST PEAK IN NEW YORK STATE...

Ryan Metcalf was both confused and yet relieved to see his son, Sean, at their front porch. Ryan had called his wife, Rita, to let her know what had transpired at the cabin. Rita had gone to the hospital upon getting the phone call to see how everyone was doing. She came back to the hospital again three days later when Sabrina gave birth to the baby. Ryan was thinking about all of this as he greeted Sean at the doorway.

Sean came into the house and was somewhat nervous as he sat down on the couch. Ryan's brother, Michael, was also at the house. Sean was surprised to see his uncle at this time. Michael had driven over from Lake Placid and he had told Ryan he had been in regular contact with Sean for the past six months.

Michael was Ryan's older brother, but he looked up to him as a surrogate father, especially after their father had vanished. Michael had always looked out for Ryan. And now he seemed to be doing the same with Sean. Ryan was somewhat envious of the situation. But it did startle Ryan somewhat that his brother had been in regular contact with Sean.

Sean took off his coat as it was rather warm in the house. Michael looked over at Sean and then said to Ryan. "Has Sean spoken to you?"

"Yes. I know he is the father of Sabrina's baby."

Michael again looked over at Sean. Sean seemed quite uncomfortable and agitated. He still would not look at his uncle. He was somewhat concerned that his uncle may have broken their confidentiality.

Michael, in a distressed manner, said, "What else did he tell you?"

"That the baby's name is Ryan Mason."

"Anything else?"

"No."

Michael saw that Sean's head had drooped. Michael hesitated but then said,

"You need to talk to Sean."

"About what?"

"He needs your help. Talk to him!"

"Why?'

Michael looked somewhat alarmed, but calmly said,

"Sean is being arrested tomorrow morning."

"For what?!"

Sean could only look at the floor. He was silent. He hoped his uncle would not say anything else. And for the moment, his uncle didn't. Sean knew he needed to tell his father what was going on. He, himself, was still not able to comprehend the situation.

CHAPTER THIRTEEN

MACOMB MOUNTAIN IS OFTEN CLIMBED BY ITSELF…

It was a cold January morning. The two Keene police officers arrived at the cabin Thursday morning at 9:45 AM. The snow continued to come down at a moderate rate. As usual, the roads were clear. The highway department employees diligently worked through the night to maintain the roads. Rarely does a snowstorm deter people getting from place to place.

The two officers approached the front door and as they did so, the door opened and Sabrina was standing before them with a colorful quilt wrapped around her.

She said, "I know why you are here. Please come in."

The taller officer spoke first, "Is Sean Metcalf here? He knows to expect us here today."

He seemed somewhat uncomfortable by the situation he had to deal with. His physical height seemed to make everything more magnified. Even though it was snowing outside the officer was not wearing an overcoat. He was in his police uniform, with a short sleeve shirt. He was well built and presented an imposing figure. That in itself was intimidating enough but the officer did not seem to use that as an advantage.

Sabrina looked over her shoulder. The baby began to cry.

"Yes. He is in the shower."

The officer looked at his partner and simply said to Sabrina, "We will wait on the front porch for him."

The officer was curt; he did not seem to want to engage in a further conversation. The taller officer's partner seemed to be quite the opposite of himself. He was short in stature, perhaps five foot six inches tall. He was dressed in a police uniform as well but wrapped in a rather large parka. The two officers could not be more of a contrast in physical appearances.

Sean appeared behind Sabrina before she could close the front door. He looked newly shaven. His hair was damp and mussed. He had put on a pair of dark blue jeans and a pull over shirt.

The smaller officer, whom Sean knew from high school, looked at Sean and stated,

“Sean Metcalf, you have a right to remain silent. Anything you say will be held against you. You have a right to counsel. If you cannot afford a lawyer one will be appointed.’

The taller officer, Sergeant Tedesco, declared,

“You are being arrested for the murder of Mr. Matthew Hamilton.”

Sean said absolutely nothing as the officer placed Sean’s hands behind his back and placed the handcuffs onto Sean’s wrists. Sean realized it would be of no good use to resist the two officers, especially Officer Tedesco who probably outweighed Sean by at least eighty pounds. The officer that had read Sean the Miranda warning, seemed somewhat embarrassed by the arrest. He would not even look at Sean.

Sabrina did not seem surprised by the events occurring before her eyes. As she held her baby in her arms she began to weep silently. She knew Sean had not murdered her father, Matthew Hamilton. But who reported to the police that Sean had done so? What possible evidence did they have to arrest Sean Metcalf?

GRANDMOTHER "MARY" METCALF

"Life is not measured by the number of breaths we take,

but by the moments that take our breath away."

The sudden disappearance of her husband, Edgar, was quite a cross for her to bear. The people of Keene were outright amazed at how strong she had been or at least appeared to be so. She knew initially she had an incredible responsibility with raising her two young sons. At the time of their father's sudden vanishing, Michael, the eldest was eleven years old and Ryan, the inquisitive one, was just five years old.

From the moment the four of them relocated to Keene from Canada, Edgar spent an incredible amount of time at the church and at various community events. Mary felt at times as though she was a single parent. She found her husband to be rather preoccupied with so many different families of Keene and their assortment of problems. Mary would sometimes mention to Edgar the need to spend more time with their sons. Edgar would almost always say he would but the reality of the scope of things was not to be true. Both Michael and Ryan would constantly ask about their father and when he would be coming home.

Deep in her heart she felt her husband was doing so much good for the community as she often heard the praises particularly after Sunday services. But she felt as if she and her husband had drifted apart. But did he feel the same way as she did? Quite often, especially during the last few weeks before Edgar went missing, she wanted to discuss with him her concerns but he would arrive home late at night most times and he would be exhausted. Most times he would sit and eat the supper Mary had prepared, get up from the table, go into the living room, watch the ten o'clock news and then go to bed. He would always be up by five thirty in the morning and depart to go to the church by six thirty. He would rarely see his two sons before he left for the day.

So when Edgar suddenly vanished, Mary was not totally overcome with shock. Many people noticed how serene she was during the ordeal. Often someone would say,

"Mary has her faith. As she has often said, "'God's will be done.'"

Mary, at the urging of Edgar, presented a series of workshops for the women of the community. Mary's love of God was evident to those around her. Her workshops emphasized a life of peace and how it could be achieved by trusting God. She would cite various scriptures to assist the respective women with their ordeals.

So when her own husband suddenly vanished she sought God's guidance. She had always placed trust in God. Weathering such a storm seemed almost inhuman. But she stay focused and heeded on the advice she presented in the workshops. Her heart though broke for her children. Michael seemed unusually quiet. At times he would exhibit a terrible moodiness; this did not surprise her as Edgar would have those streaks in himself as well. Whereas, Michael was quite the opposite. He would constantly inquire as to what happened to his father. He would often repeat what different people had to say about his father.

Mary knew she had to show a good example to her sons. She was now their only immediate role model. She knew she had built a solid foundation of faith. She could only hope the same would be true for her two sons.

But now she knew she had to make some difficult decisions. One of them was deciding where to live if Keene was not to be the place. She could return to Canada but in an amazingly short period of time, as they had only been in Keene for a year before Edgar disappeared, she had made many acquaintances. Many of these fine people came to her assistance when this terrible ordeal began.

CHAPTER FOURTEEN

BASIN MOUNTAIN IS VERY CHALLENGING WITH STEEP ROCKS AND NARROW LEDGES...

The village of Keene has a number of shops along with a Stewart's convenience store and gas station, a post office, a bank, a garden center, a car repair shop, a print shop and a fire house, which was relocated and upgraded after a horrific hurricane-like storm had hit the region.Many of the business establishments had been started by longtime residents of the community.

The police scanner went off at Lou's Printing Shop. Lou had opened up his shop in Keene over twenty years ago. Lou seemed to know just about every person in Keene. He had also made acquaintances with some of the seasonal residents.

People were always impressed with Lou's talent for being able to create all sorts of items requested. He was in the middle of putting together the wedding invitations for Mayor Galente's daughter's wedding.

Lou stopped what he was doing and listened to the message.

"Arrest made at Mountainside Road. Address: 22 Mountainside Road. Mr. Sean Metcalf arrested for the homicide of Matthew Hamilton."

Lou abruptly stopped what he was working on. He began to sweat as he wondered what he had heard. He wished he could listen to the message again that had been transmitted. What was going on? Matthew Hamilton had drowned a few months ago. At least that is what Lou always thought to be true. The dispatcher message would carry quickly to the Keene residents. Lou knew the people of Keene would be upset by this news! It was baffling.

He needed to make his way to the mayor's office as upon calling the town hall he was informed a news conference was scheduled for eleven o'clock. That seemed rather hastyas the scanner message had just been broadcast at nine fifty five this morning; this was just a little over an hour away.

Lou called his wife, Mildred, to let her know of the latest development, especially since Sean is her nephew.

Mildred seemed out of breath when she responded to Lou's call, "I know. It's on the local news station!"

"Can you believe it?"

"No. It seems impossible. Someone must have been misinformed."

"I know. But we do not know what the reasons are they have to arrest Sean."

"I understand, but I am very upset."

"Do you want me to come home?"

"No. That is alright. Go to the news conference."

"Okay. I love you.'

"I love you too. Be safe."

Lou hung up the phone. He grabbed his coat and checked to see if his car keys were in his pocket. He took them out and proceeded to his car, which was covered with a couple of inches of newly fallen snow. He was having a tough time concentrating on clearing the car of snow. This news was very odd. It was also very troubling. He knew this would cause such angst for Anna Hamilton. He could not truly comprehend the situation. And he knew the Metcalf family must be devastated.

CHAPTER FIFTEEN

DONALDSON MOUNTAIN IS THE PEAK LOCATED IN THE MIDDLE OF THE HIGH PEAKS RANGE...

As Lou got into his car to warm it up, the Lake Placid radio station was reporting the arrest of Sean Metcalf. Lou continued to clear the snow off his car. The snow had stopped falling. Lou made his way to the town hall. He knew many of the Keene residents by name and he could only assume that many of them would be in attendance at the town hall.

The winds were picking up and the sun had emerged. But the sun did not take away the chill in the air. The high peaks behind Mayor Galente's office were glimmering from the newly fallen snowfall.

Quite a crowd had gathered for the eleven o'clock news conference being held in the small courtroom. Keene townspeople were not used to this type of an event. Some of the shopkeepers had closed their businesses so they could attend the news conference. They realized their chances of having customers visit their shops were slim. No one could recall the last time a news conference of this proportion had been held. The room was set up with fifty chairs; every seat was occupied. A few news stations had set up their cameras, including a NBC-TV affiliate, along the side two aisles. A podium had been placed in front of the judge's elevated desk.

Mayor Galente proceeded to the podium at eleven o'clock sharp. He was known as a man to always start everything on time. His bi-weekly village hall meetings were run in an efficient manner. They were always well-organized. The meetings were hardly ever prolonged as a strict agenda was always followed. The people of Keene came to respect that format.

A few of the residents could not be accommodated inside the courtroom, so they stood outside so they could listen to the proceedings. The weather did not seem to deter them from being there.

Galente was a small man, approximately five feet, four inches tall. He weighed one hundred and thirty five pounds. He was dressed in a grey three piece suit with a white dress shirt and red tie. This was his usual garb. He looked quite debonair. He did not though feel comfortable with the spotlight upon himself. It was not his nature to have the spotlight focused on him, but he knew it was his duty to conduct the briefing. Mayor Galente could not wait until this news conference was over.

He cleared his throat more out of nervousness than anything else and then began to speak,

"Good morning."

His voice was rather deep and loud, quite surprising for an individual of such small stature. His voice signaled that he was in command. And this was also respected by the townspeople.

"Thank you for coming on such short notice. Earlier today, Mr. Sean Metcalf had been taken into custody and arraigned for the murder of Mr. Matthew Hamilton."

The full capacity crowd was very quiet. Not a sound could be heard both inside and outside the courtroom.

"Mr. Metcalf has been detained and will be transferred to the county jail in Elizabethtown. I have nothing further to report as Mr. Metcalf is in the process of consulting with his lawyer."

The people in the courtroom became rather restless. There was a loud murmur from the crowd. Many of the people wondered why a news conference would be scheduled if the mayor did not have much information, in fact little at all, to share with the crowd.

A voice could be heard above the noise, "Who is that? Who is the lawyer?"

The voice was that of a local news reporter. Mayor Galente turned to the young man and said,

"His name is Madison Schultz."

"The local historian?"

"Yes." Mayor Galente started to depart but then stopped again.

"I have nothing else to say. I'm sorry."

Galente left through a back door behind the judge's desk. There was a lot of shouting and speculating by the crowd. A lady could be heard saying, "I thought Matthew Hamilton drowned back in August. I went to the funeral!"

Many residents were coming to the realization that they felt the same way as the lady who had spoken her thoughts out loud.

SABRINA MESIER

"Hope is a good thing, perhaps the best of things."

Sabrina was the daughter of Sid Mesier and the step daughter of Matthew Hamilton. She adored her father but never really associated with her stepfather. Her stepfather had seemed distant at times. Sometimes she pondered as to what Matthew Hamilton was up to. She often wondered how well she treated her mother. And that had greatly concerned her over the years.

Her dad was a true gentleman. He always seemed to have the right advice no matter what the situation might be. He was also a simple man. In Sabrina's eyes he never wanted anything outlandish. He just wanted his daughter and wife to have everything he could provide for them. And that he did. He was not a selfish man either. People often sought him out for advice. Sid was a patient individual. No person's concern became trivial to Sid. Even if he could not solve a person's dilemma he always was able to provide comfort. Many thought he should have been a counselor or perhaps even a priest. Sabrina was glad Sid was her dad.

But in Sabrina's eyes, Matthew Hamilton was quite the opposite. She felt he had become interested in her mother in a very short while after her Sabrina's father had passed away. It seemed odd that Matthew became interested in her mom right after details of Anna's inheritance from Sid were released in the local newspaper. Sid had left behind a wealth of real estate along with a one million dollar insurance policy. The policy was paid out to Anna within two months of Sid's death as no foul play was assumed to have occurred.

Sabrina was skeptical, to say the least, about Matthew Hamilton. She tried to broach the subject with her mom a few times but to no avail. In Sabrina's eyes Matthew seemed to be somewhat shady and mysterious. Sabrina, though, believed that her mom was an intelligent enough individual to not allow Matthew to swindle her of her wealth. Sabrina, at times, thought her mom might be somewhat naïve to Matthew's doings, or better yet his manipulation.

When Matthew was reported to have died, this news did not really upset Sabrina. Her mom on the other hand was devastated as now she had lost not one but two husbands. Sabrina was overwhelmed by the incredible support the people of Keene and the surrounding area had shown them. This is when she met a young man named Sean Metcalf. He was a handsome, down-to-earth individual. She was impressed by both his warm personality and good looks. He was not pompous or obnoxious. He was a real gentleman. Sabrina never thought she would meet someone like Sean in her own hometown.

Sabrina was aware of the Metcalf family. Mr. Metcalf was a well respected resident of Keene. Mrs. Metcalf was an avid volunteer in the community. Over the years she knew of their son, Sean, but did not really get to know him until her stepfather's death was reported. She felt very comfortable talking to Sean about the details of her life. Sean likewise felt the same way. Within days they fell in love with one another. Both Anna and Rita and Ryan Metcalf were delighted.

CHAPTER SIXTEEN

EAST DIX HAS BEEN RENAMED GRACE PEAK, IN COMMEMORATION OF THE FIRST WOMAN TO CLIMB THE 46 HIGH PEAKS (1937)…

Sean woke up the next morning just as a corrections officer came into the courtroom outside the jail cells. Sean had a very restless night. He had hardly slept; maybe, at best, he dozed for twenty-minute intervals. He was stunned by the sudden turn of events. He did not quite understand how he could have been charged with such a crime. His father was due to meet with him at 9:15 AM so they could attend a bail hearing.

Sean knew the charges were ridiculous yet here he was locked in an Elizabethtown jail cell. Out loud he said to himself, "Did Sabrina's mother tell the police I murdered her husband? Why?"

He was feeling ill; his stomach had a pain in it. The entire town truly thought Matthew Hamilton had drowned. Sean could not even speculate as to who was trying to place the burden of the murder of Matthew Hamilton upon him. Why would Sabrina's mother do this? That was impossible. Who was seeking revenge upon the Hamilton family? He could not think of a single individual. But somebody was trying to make it look as though Sean committed a murder.

The snow was coming down quickly. Another storm had approached the area early in the morning. For the first time in over ten years, schools were closed. The local radio station weather forecaster had predicted an additional fifteen to eighteen inches of snow by nightfall. Sean could see the snow coming down from a high window inside his cell. Sean's father still had not arrived by ten o'clock. There suddenly was a flash of light and the electricity went off. The corrections officer quickly came to Sean's cell. In addition, a drunkard had just been placed in a cell across from Sean but the new arrival was too despondent to notice the loss of electricity. The jail cells were electronically activated so the officer led Sean to the waiting area.

The corrections officer used his cell phone to inform his supervisor of the loss of electricity. He then got off the phone and instructed Sean to follow him into the courtroom. He then instructed Sean to sit at the defense lawyer's table. He proceeded to handcuff Sean to the immoveable chair. It seemed to Sean that this was a little excessive.

The officer was doing what he was told to do by his superior. Sean could tell that the officer did not agree with having to handcuff Sean to the table. Sean knew the officer by name but he was hesitant to engage in any type of conversation. The officer left the court room to go and tend to the drunkard he had left in the jail cell. This person could do no harm as he had been in a deep sleep ever since he was placed in the cell. He reeked of liquor and stale cigarettes. Sean was happy to not have to share the cell with the drunkard. That was his only immediate relief.

Sean could now get a much better view out one of the side windows of the courtroom. The snow was coming down so hard he could not see the mountains. He wondered if his father would ever be able to get to the court for the bail hearing. Sean knew he could not spend another night in a jail cell. He felt as if he was locked in the cell for more than a week. The cell consisted of a bunk bed along with a small sink and a rather dirty toilet. In addition, he had to deal with the stench of the drunkard placed in the adjacent cell.

A side door opened and the court clerk entered. She walked over to Sean, looked down at the handcuffs, then looked back up at Sean and said, "Mr. Metcalf, your father and your lawyer will arrive momentarily. They just called the judge's cell phone to inform us."

"Thank you.'

The clerk then walked over to her desk and sorted out some papers. The back door of the courtroom opened. Sean looked over his shoulder expecting to see his father. Instead Sabrina entered the courtroom. Her burgundy coat was covered with snow. She removed her scarf and sat down. She was a few rows away from Sean, She did not look over at him. The lights suddenly came back on. Sean could see her more clearly and noticed she had been crying. He thought to himself, what is really going on with this whole situation that Sabrina has not told him. He hoped his dad would arrive. And then he did along with another individual, Mr. Schultz.

CHAPTER SEVENTEEN

IROQUOIS PEAK IS OFTEN CLIMBED WITH ALGONQUIN PEAK AND WRIGHT PEAK…

The judge entered the courtroom. He was a rather large man, weighing at least three hundred pounds. He wore an immense black robe. A navy blue tie and white collared shirt could be seen as the robe was not zippered up to the judge's neck. The judge possessed a bellowing voice. No one was going to tangle with this man. But people knew of him as a gentle soul. Many residents said his bark is bigger than his bite. Nevertheless Sean still feared the judge.

"Before us today we have a bail hearing for Sean Metcalf. I believe one hundred thousand dollars is about to be posted?"

"That is correct," stated Mr. Schultz, Sean's lawyer. The judge knew him more so as the Keene historian. The judge seemed a little puzzled by the involvement of Mr. Schultz with the case. The judge knew Schultz to be an astute man but not in the field of court proceedings. Schultz had published various books on the history of the Adirondacks. He was an expert on the region's history. But the judge never knew he had a license to practice law or for that matter to frequent the court with a client of interest. The judge even went as far to ask Mr. Schulz to present his law license so he could validate Schulz's presence as the legal representation for Sean Metcalf.

Sean's father was seated right behind Sean. Ryan placed his hand on Sean's right shoulder. Sean was trembling somewhat. His hands were cuffed behind his back. This was normal procedure for a bail hearing. He was extremely anxious as to what decision the judge would make. The judge seemed to pause for an inordinate amount of time as he looked around the courtroom as about eighteen to twenty people were in attendance. This seemed rather unusual as the bail hearing was only scheduled this morning. In addition, the roads were rather treacherous.

The judge cleared his throat, took a sip of water from the glass on his desk and then announced,

"I will grant the bail request if the county district attorney does not have any reservation."

A well-dressed young lady shook her head and presented no objection. The judge continued,

"Okay, Sean Metcalf must stay at his father's residence and will be placed under house arrest."

The judge hit his gavel on the desk, stood up and departed. It took a few moments for the judge to remove his immense body from behind the desk.

Sean, his father and the lawyer, Mr. Schultz left the courtroom and descended into the basement, led by the court clerk. The basement area smelled musty and it was cluttered with old pieces of furniture. Most of it look as if it was ready to be disposed. The clerk unlocked the handcuffs from behind Sean's back. The clerk then placed a monitor on Sean's right ankle. The clerk proceeded to explain the parameters of the ankle bracelet restrictions. Sean half listened to the information provided by the clerk. Sean was anxious to depart and return to his parent's house. He was becoming agitated. He was also rather hungry which surprised him especially with the current circumstances.

The clerk also instructed the three of them to depart through a back doorway so they could avoid any press representatives that might be waiting for them to exit the front of the building. Ryan thought that was somewhat considerate of the clerk to advise them to do so. They climbed into Ryan's SUV and drove out of the small parking lot. One reporter tried to gain Sean's attention but to no avail as he was seated in the back seat and Mr. Schultz rode in the front passenger seat. The reporter chased the vehicle down the road and even tried to take a picture with his cell phone but to no avail. The roads were covered with snow and visibility was quite limited. The reporter stopped running as he feared he would slip and fall.

REVEREND METCALF

"Change in life is inevitable."

THIRTY YEARS AGO

It had been eighteen years since Reverend Edgar Metcalf had planned his disappearance from Keene in upstate New York. He had arrived in Keene with his wife and two sons. He had been selected to be the pastor of the region's congregation. Even though he appeared to assimilate well into the community he was feeling a sense of unease. He loved his wife and children but he felt something was missing in his life.

Immediately upon his arrival the residents of Keene warmly welcomed him and his family. There were weekly luncheons after the Sunday services. People frequented the parson bearing gifts, tokens and advice, and mostly gossip, about the community's daily life. He seemed to be receptive to the kindness but deep inside he found it all to be very distracting. He knew he could not last in the area. What conflicted him though was to see how happy his wife and two sons had become with their new life.

Edgar tried to express his thoughts to his wife but to no avail. Sometimes when he would begin a conversation to discuss his feelings, one thing would lead to another and they would discuss other items of interest. His wife often would repeat much of the news and gossip he had already heard from church members. He found this to be quite annoying.

So eighteen years ago he departed one day after telling his wife he was going to the library. Instead he was able to hitch a series of rides into Lake Placid, bought a bus ticket and made his way to a rural area outside of Toronto. He knew of the area from correspondence with a high school friend who had settled down there. But Reverend Metcalf never connected with the friend. Instead he met a woman, who was in her thirties, asked her to marry him and they had twin daughters together. Reverend Metcalf never made an attempt to reconnect with his first wife and two sons, who at this time were twenty nine and twenty three years of age.

The reverend was always concerned that someday one of them would find him, especially his younger son, Ryan. Even at the early age of five, Ryan was inquisitive. He was also aware that his son had become a detective after deciding to go to college for a law enforcement degree. Reverend Metcalf knew he would have to stay alert and find ways to keep current on the happenings of the family he left behind.

CHAPTER EIGHTEEN

PRESENT DAY

MOUNT MARCY IS THE TALLEST MOUNTAIN IN NEW YORK STATE…

The County Medical Examiner ordered the immediate exhumation of Matthew Hamilton's body. He ordered this because now there was a suspect that had been arrested in the murder of Matthew Hamilton. Oddly enough the person arrested and charged with the homicide of Matthew Hamilton was Sean Metcalf. Sean's father had often been called upon to provide necessary services when a criminal investigation was taking place. How ironic that Ryan Metcalf's son had been arrested.

The County Medical Examiner had discovered that an autopsy was not performed at the time of Matthew Hamilton's death. The Medical Examiner felt he needed to take some control over the mesmerizing situation. He hoped the newly appointed coroner would use his jurisdiction to remedy matters.

The entire situation was quite baffling. He wondered why the coroner did not require an autopsy to be performed as Hamilton's death should have been labeled as a mysterious death. The coroner knew that was standard procedure. He wanted to give the prior coroner the benefit of the doubt so until he researched an explanation he waited to make a judgment on the case. But what he feared was that no reasonable explanation would be found. And that is not something he wanted to tackle as then the prior coroner's reputation would come into question.

This was not agreed upon by Mrs. Hamilton but she did not really have any jurisdiction over the matter as the situation had now become a criminal investigation. The Keene Cemetery workers brought the coffin up from the grave. It took quite a few hours to dig off the snow which was at least twenty inches deep. Due to the harsh winter the area was experiencing, the ground was rather frozen so special heated equipment was needed to reach the coffin which was not buried as deep as originally estimated. The coffin oddly enough was only four feet deep into the ground.

Upon lifting the coffin from the ground it was placed on a flatbed truck and brought to the funeral home. The coffin was lighter than expected as only three men were needed to lift it up onto the flatbed. The coffin was then transferred to the funeral home hearse and transported to the medical center in nearby Elizabethtown.

****

Meanwhile, Sean had been eating breakfast, or as much of it as he could, at his parent's house. He had no choice but to be there as the judge had placed a mandate on his bail for him to stay at his parent's house. Sean's mom had prepared him a stack of pancakes along with both link sausage and bacon. The chain of events in the last twenty-four hours was staggering. Sean continued to state his innocence.

A knock was heard at the front door. Sean looked at the door but did not get up to respond to the knock. Sean's dad opened the door and standing on the front porch was Mr. Sydney Emerson, a prominent town lawyer. Mr. Emerson was also a close family friend of the Metcalfs.

"Good morning to all of you!"

Mr. Emerson weighed approximately two hundred and seventy five pounds; he reminded many people of President William Taft. Emerson's posture was rather debonair. His slick black hair portrayed him in a rather favorable fashion. He was known throughout the community of being a shrewd lawyer. Most lawyers in the region did not want to have the opportunity to oppose him. Emerson's family has long roots in the Keene community. His grandfather and great uncle were longtime employees of the Westing Mining Operation. They helped to pave the roadway to Elizabethtown in 1912.

Emerson's reputation preceded him. Emerson seemed to know every person not only in Keene, but the surrounding towns as well. If a person came into some difficulties with the law, Emerson would almost always be recommended as the counsel to contact. Sometimes he would reduce or even waiver his fees to take on a case of interest. But that did not occur too often. Some wondered how Emerson would pick and choose his fees. Some were baffled as to how he received so many cases. It was as if he had a monopoly on the legal field.

Sean was happy to see Mr. Emerson, as was Sean's father.

"So, what do we have before us?"

"Well, it seems the Hamilton family is now saying Sean killed Mr. Hamilton. And it does not make any sense!"

Mr. Emerson did not seem at all bothered by what Sean's father was reporting to him.

"Do not worry. We will sort everything out. Your prior lawyer, Mr. Schultz, graciously gave me a framework of what has transpired thus far"

Emerson paused and then continued,

"Schultz knew he was over his head with this case.'

If nothing else, Emerson could be bold and somewhat candid when he spoke his mind. He did not seem to ever beat around the bush. His blunt manner more than likely brought him great success as an attorney. None of the Metcalfs really questioned Mr. Schultz's decision to excuse himself from the case. Schultz had not directly informed the Metcalfs of his decision.

Emerson then asked to use the Metcalf's landlinetelephone as he knew his cell phone would not have reception at this altitude. Emerson proceeded to sit down in a large chair to accommodate his bulk and then made a series of phone calls. He made himself comfortable in the chair by the roaring fireplace.

CHAPTER NINETEEN

MOUNT COLVIN WAS NAMED AFTER VERPLANK COLVIN, THE GREAT SURVEYOR OF THE ADIRONDACK PARK...

Upon completing his telephone calls Mr. Emerson told Sean's father he had spoken again to Mr. Schultz. He informed Sean that Mr. Schultz could no longer formally be the counsel for the case. The judge's clerk had just received approval from the judge. Mr. Emerson continued to say there are many details to discuss about the case.

Naturally, Sean's father was a little concerned with the legal fees Emerson would charge. Ryan did not want to discuss this matter in front of Sean or his wife for that matter. Ryan had the necessary funds to retain Emerson but he was still concerned what Emerson would expect to receive in legal fees.He also realized he would do everything he could to provide the necessary support to defend his son, even if he had to take out a second mortgage on their home. The money issue was truly secondary to him. He knew his wife would feel the same way. Ryan was very aware of Emerson's reputation to gain victories with practically all of his cases he took up. Due to that reason he knew Emerson would not spare the Metcalf family any type of reduced fees. But Ryan understood his son needed the very best lawyer to deal with the extraordinary situation.

Emerson said to both Sean and Sean's father,

"The body of Matthew Hamilton was exhumed. The coffin was transported by the KeeneCemetery workers to Elizabethtown."

Emerson paused and asked both of them to sit down. Sean was concerned about the manner that which Emerson seemed to have further news of interest. Sean's mother, Rita, came through the front doorway with a few shopping bags. Ryan got up immediately and assisted his wife. Emerson walked over to Rita and gave her a kiss. Rita knew Emerson rather well and seemed to be somewhat relieved that he was there to discuss the case with all of them. Rita also knew by hiring Emerson as the legal counsel for Sean it would come with a hefty price. But this was not the time to concern herself with that matter. Rita looked over to her husband, Ryan, realizing he had the same thoughts pass his mind. He hoped her son's case would be resolved in quick fashion not only due to the legal fees but more importantly so her son could get on with his life. The entire situation was excruciating for all of them.

All of them sat down, including Rita, in the living room. Ryan filled in Rita on what Mr. Emerson had told them thus far. Emerson then continued, rather hesitantly,

"The District Attorney's office has just informed me that when they opened Matthew Hamilton's coffin, there was no body inside of it."

Sean and his parents were aghast. No one said a word. Sean even more startled than anyone else as he had seen the inside of Matthew Hamilton's coffin and there was a body inside of it at that time.

****

The local newspaper reporter had just left a message on the voicemail of the Metcalf's telephone just as Mr. Emerson informed Sean, Ryan and Rita of the coffin status. The reporter had simply said,

"My name is Wade Kapler. Please call me at the Lake Placid News office. My telephone number will appear on your caller identification screen. I'd like to get your reaction to the reports of a missing body. Your comments would be appreciated."

Sydney Emerson was not surprised by the turn of events as he knew the Hamilton family had numerous incidents occur over the past few years. The Metcalf family looked both baffled and frightened. Emerson explained that he had defended one of the Hamilton nephews a few years back.

Spencer Hamilton was accused of breaking and entering into a local gift shop. The case never came to trial as Emerson presented numerous inconsistencies with the police reports. Ironically, it was a rarity if any of Emerson's cases ever went to trial. Many felt that the opposing lawyer was intimidated by Emerson's prowess. He was an overpowering and intimidating individual. He could often persuade even a judge to see his side of things. People realized he was a real slick lawyer and one that could almost always swing a case in his client's favor.

But the idea that the coffin of Matthew Hamilton being empty would only cause everybody to speculate as to what had occurred. Did Matthew Hamilton drown? Was his body stolen? And if that was the case, for what reason?

Ryan interrupted Emerson by asking.

"What does that have to do with Sean's situation? I do not understand the connection."

Emerson continued to say,
"You'll see."

Sean looked rather frightened. Both of his parents noticed that their son was becoming rather upset by the situation. One bizarre thing after another seemed to be occurring. Emerson, though, seemed rather calm and collected as if he was reporting the weather to the Metcalf family.

The latest scenario with the Hamilton family was quite different. An outsider would call it bizarre. How could Matthew Hamilton's body be missing? Where was it? Could he be alive?

CHAPTER TWENTY

MOUNT SKYLIGHT HAS IMPRESSIVE VIEWS OF OVER THIRTY OTHER HIGH PEAKS…

The Keene police department consisted of two part time officers, one full time officer and a police chief. The county coroner's office had informed the Police Chief that he needed to come over to the Elizabethtown coroner's office. The coroner's office was located at the government building on Main Street. Mark Winston, the Keene Police Chief, who was also the senior officer, arrived at the coroner's office at ten o'clock in the morning He parked his car in the side parking lot. As he exited his car he was greeted by a few different people he had known from his other visits to the county government office. One in particular was the local hardware store owner. Winston knew him for over twenty five years. In fact, Winston worked for the proprietor for a few years before he got married. The hardware store owner asked Winston how he was doing.

"Hi Mark. I hope you and your family are hanging in there."

"Mr. Smith, it is so good to see you. We are doing okay. I am sure you have heard about the odd case we are dealing with."

"Yes. I know you will bring it to a resolution. You always have had the ability to figure out a case, particularly the real questionable situations."

"Thank you. I have to go as I have a meeting with the coroner. I'll call you. We'd love to have you and your wife over the house for dinner"

"That would be great. Take care. Be safe."

"You too."

Mark Winston had been a lifelong resident of Keene. His mother's family had been builders of cottages in Keene during the 1880's and 1890's. So his family had a long history in the Adirondacks. It was a place he never thought about leaving. Most of his days on the job were rather peaceful and uneventful. So this situation had become rather troubling to the police chief and others as well. His own children were being pestered in school as to what was going on.

Winston entered the coroner's office and was greeted by the secretary, Selma Griffin. Selma immediately recognized police Chief Winston and said,

"Hello Chief Winston. It is so nice to see you again."

"Hello Selma. I wish it was under different circumstances."

Selma looked to engage Winston in further conversation but she knew this was hardly the time to do so.

"Here is the report the coroner wanted you to read."

"Thank you."

Winston, forty-two years old, married, and the father of three children, one son and two daughters, sat at a corner table and began to peruse the report. Chief Winston's wife had warned him to be calm with the situation. She was always concerned with his health. Just last year he had experienced chest pains. She gently reminded him that his father had suffered a massive heart attack at the age of forty four. The family had a long history of coronary ailments. Winston religiously met with his doctor every six months. His wife would never allow him to miss his regularly scheduled appointment.

The coroner's report was only three pages in length. It only took Winston less than ten minutes to not only read the report but reread it as well. As he finished up reading the document he looked up and the coroner was standing next to him.

“Good morning sir.”

“Good morning Chief Winston. Thank you for coming over today.”

The coroner asked the police chief to come into his office. Once seated, the police chief asked,

“So what does this mean about Matthew Hamilton’s body missing?’

The coroner hesitated and then said,

“Well, my initial findings show that Matthew Hamilton’s body was never placed in the coffin.”

Winston looked puzzled but did not say anything. During his tenure as the police chief, not much really startled him. The worst case he had to handle occurred a few years ago. He and a colleague were called to a horrific scene. An elderly husband and wife had been quarreling for a few hours on a hot summer day. Things became rather complicated between the two of them. The husband had accused his physically disabled wife of seeing another man.

When Winston and his young police officer came upon the scene, the husband was chopping wood even though it was eighty two degrees. Across the yard sat his wife’s body. She had been decapitated. Her head was sitting on a nearby picnic table. The young officer immediately began to vomit as soon as he spotted the headless woman.

So Police Chief Winston was prepared for any type of news from the coroner. The coroner continued,

“In fact, Chief Winston, a death certificate is not on file at the County Medical Examiner’s office.”

“Are you telling me Hamilton is alive?’

“First, I do not know that at this time. Second, as you know, I just took over as coroner ten days ago.” It had been a rather frantic first ten days of the new coroner’s tenure. So many loose ends and open files had been left after the sudden death of his predecessor.

The coroner hesitated for a moment but then said, “And third, an autopsy was not only not performed it was not ordered as well. That violates the required protocol of this office.”

Winston knew the coroner was newly appointed as the longtime coroner, Alexander Stevord, died three weeks ago. The new coroner continued,

“I am only telling you Matthew Hamilton’s body was never placed in the coffin. And as you realize it is not my role to investigate why. I will need to review Mr. Stevord’s notes of interest to determine the details of this case. I know I can count on your patience as I research further information of interest.”

Winston found himself lost in thought. He knew the case had become more complicated. He reflected upon the words of wisdom Mr. Smith had given to him out at the parking lot. Winston realized he needed to be provided more details of the situation so he could proceed with a more thorough investigation. He needed to go back to the day and time when Matthew Hamilton was declared dead. He needed to contact who knew what at the time in question. Winston’s thoughts were disrupted by a bit of a commotion coming from the outer office.

The door to the coroner’s office suddenly opened with a loud ruckus. Standing before Winston and the coroner was Emerson. Emerson had obviously bypassed the coroner’s secretary.Selma Griffin was right behind Emerson looking to apologize to her boss, but the coroner knew it was no fault of Selma's that Emerson abruptly entered the office. He knew his secretary had no way of stopping Emerson.

In a bellowing voice Emerson said,

"What is going on? Why haven't I been informed of the situation?"

Leering at the coroner and the police chief, Emerson blurted,

"Is there something you need to tell me about?"

Emerson's physical size was overwhelming in the small office space. The coroner just simply said, "Who are you sir?"

Emerson could hardly contain himself and pronounced, "I am Sydney Emerson. You are obviously new around here!"

The coroner simply said, "Yes I am. And I am sure once you calm down, we can engage in a civilized discussion." Emerson was not used to a person challenging him. Emerson was not sure what to do next.

PAUL PIPFORD

"Hope is eternal."

Paul Pipford had relocated to the Keene Valley area when he was twenty-two years old. He opened a small shop that catered to the avid hikers of the High Peaks region. It was not a surprise to many of the locals that Paul's shop became a rather quick success. Paul exhibited his rather extensive knowledge of hiking tips but also his rather vast array of information about the high peaks trails. In fact, Pipford was listed as a 46er. He had hiked all forty six of the high peaks trails. He had frequented two of the trails he particularly enjoyed. Those were Mount Marcy and Wright Peak. He particularly found Wright Peak to be a fascinating place to hike regardless of the time of year.

Pipford did not seem to have any family ties to the area. Some wondered why he settled in Keene Valley yet that did not deter people from welcoming him to the community. One thing Pipford enjoyed doing was taking people on hiking expeditions. Again any person that went on a hiking adventure with Paul were astounded by his knowledge of the respective trail's background.

One resident who enjoyed Paul's hiking adventures was the Keene Police Chief Mark Winston. Winston found Paul Pipford to be a fascinating individual. Winston did not want to pry too much but he always wondered why such a young man, who was single and no family in the area, decided to settle in the Keene Valley region. But Winston never asked Pipford. Winston sometimes wondered if Pipford had really hiked all forty six of the High Peaks. But he did not put much thought into it.

Pipford was not only an experienced hiker but an avid historian. He was very interested in the history of Wright Peak. On January 16, 1962, a nighttime B-47 training flight crashed just north of the 4587 footsummit. Four airmen lost their lives in the crash. They were flying in bad weather.Blizzard conditions on the often windy peak made it impossible to bring the bodies down for several days after the January 21 spotting of the wreckage.

It was believed that they thought they had cleared the High Peaks and were approaching the Plattsburgh Air Force base. But they slammed into Wright Peak. Some parts of the ill-fated aircraft are still scattered around the area close to the top of the mountain. Whenever Pipford took a group to the area he explained in detail the plight of the B-47 crash. He knew the backgrounds of each of the four men that perished.

Pipford was also rather astute with some of the history of Mount Marcy. As some people knew, probably the most often repeated story about the ascent of Marcy. It was the ascent made by Theodore Roosevelt and his group in September 1901. After Roosevelt and the rest of them left the summit they decided to eat lunch by a lake. A guide came rushing up to report that President William McKinley, who had been shot by an assassin a week earlier in Buffalo, was dying. Pipford would always tell this story with such dramatic flair. Pipford's reputation as a charismatic hiking guide quickly became the talk of the region. Pipford would then always show where all of this took place and then he would proceed to describe how Roosevelt rushed by foot down the trail and then by horse and wagon drove through the night to the North Creek railroad station. Pipford would then emotionally describe that Roosevelt was informed that McKinley had died. Teddy Roosevelt had become the president of the United States. Police Chief Winston was always enthralled by Pipford's accuracy for details. And he had gone on this venture three different times.

But what fascinated Winston even more was the startling arrest he had to make of Paul Pipford approximately three years after Pipford had settled down in the Keene Valley area. Winston arrested Pipford for a double homicide. The residents of Keene and Keene Valley were horrified.

PART THREE

CHAPTER TWENTY*ONE

FORTY-EIGHT YEARS EARLIER

WRIGHT PEAK IS NUMBER ONE FOR WIND FACTOR…

Alexander Stevord had always lived in the Adirondacks. Only once did he travel outside the region and that was to assist with an autopsy in Vermont. His family's roots in the area dated back to the 1840's, when a fledging iron industry existed in Keene. His grandfather and father had been the past two individuals to hold the county coroner position. Upon Alex's father's sudden death, Alex became the youngest coroner at the age of thirty-two. The position was an appointed office. Most municipalities in New York State appointed the county coroner. It was rare for the public to elect the coroner. The mayor, who was actually Alex's uncle, figured it was just as easy to appoint Alex as a third generation Stevord to be the coroner. No one from the five people, all male county board objected to the mayor's decision to appoint Alex as the coroner. Behind closed doors politicking was a common practice.

Most residents were not aware of the deals made by the different government officials. Many items of interest were either kept quiet or squashed. The public for the most part did not get involved in the daily happenings of the government system. There really never seemed to be much interaction with the public. The town meetings were usually held every other Tuesday at eleven o'clock in the morning. Thus most of the male citizenry was either at the factories or the farms tending their jobs. The females were usually at home tending to the children and the regular house chores.

The Stevord family had a long history of keeping incidents close to the vest. Different times a call would come in that a person had died in a home. In quick fashion, the body would be transported, a death certificate would be issued and the family buried the body. This became regular procedure in these parts especially if there were questionable circumstances. One time the long time local restaurant owner's teenage son was found dead in the family's garage. When the restaurant owner opened his garage one morning he found his son dead in the front seat of the car. The local residents realized the restaurant owner's son had probably suffocated to death from the carbon monoxide fumes that had gathered from the running car in the closed garage.

If the media ever asked the coroner, who was a Stevord, for a comment, none would be given. Usually an office secretary would simply say,

"I am sorry. Mr. Sevord is not available at this time to comment on the matter at hand."

And the reporter would then place that exact quote in in his article. This was the routine and he had not changed no matter what the situation or incident was at the time. Even though the reporter would look to enforce the first amendment rights of freedom of the press, it did not change the response of the coroner's.

Alex Stevord was known to frequent the local tavern. He never seemed to heed to his grandfather's philosophy of "Loose lips sinks ships." As Stevord would become somewhat intoxicated after engaging in five beers and chasers, he was known to openly discuss the most recent case he was dealing with at his office. Surprisingly none of the details of his alcohol induced discussions made its way to the local newspaper. Even the local reporter would come by and listen to Stevord's rambling. But the reporter knew he could not print the information he would hear as some of Stevord's cronies would intimidate the reporter with their verbal and sometimes physical bullying. This was small town politics at its worst. The old time residents, in particular, were very protective of Alex Stevord and his doings. It was almost like nepotism was rampant.

PRESENT DAY

After serving as the County Coroner for forty-eight years, Alexander Stevord was found dead in his car at the Elizabethtown government offices' parking lot by two men. They were entering the main entrance when they noticed Mr. Stevord's head slumped over the steering wheel of his car and the vehicle was still running. One of the men ran inside and notified the receptionist seated at the lobby desk. She called the police station and a police car and an ambulance came onto the scene within a few minutes.

Alex was already dead. He had suffered a massive heart attack. His body was still warm. He had no next of kin. He had always been single, even though he had a longtime girlfriend. The mayor appointed an interim coroner upon being informed of Alex's sudden death. And, ironically, no autopsy was ordered to be performed. A death certificate was quickly signed and Alex Stevord was put to rest three days after his funeral.

His two day wake was held at the Elizabethtown funeral home. The line was long throughout the two day wake. People came from all over the Adirondack region to pay respects for the longtime coroner. Visitors included the governor of New York State and the catholic bishop of the region. The funeral mass was over ninety minutes long. The church was packed and people stood outside to hear the service. The priest presiding over the funeral service was a longtime friend of the Stevord family. His homily was over thirty minutes in length. He spoke about Alex Stevord as if Stevord was a saint. The priest's stories were quite amusing. The priest also emphasized Alex Stevord's love of God and that he was a daily communicant. The burial was privately done a week later. He was laid to rest at the Keene Cemetery next to his parents.

And for the first time in quite a long time there was no Stevord family member to appoint as the county coroner.

CHAPTER TWENTY*TWO

NYE MOUNTAIN IS A SHORT SIDE TRIP TO A NEARBY VIEWLESS SUMMIT…

The new county coroner, James Boyler, was not taken back at all by Sydney Emerson's abrupt response. It seemed as not much would rattle Boyler. And Emerson could be quite a handful. Prior to Police Chief Winston's arrival, Boyler had read a detailed account written by Alex Stevord. Stevord had left a year-by-year journal since he became coroner forty-eight years ago. In a recent journal entry, Stevord scribed,

"That lawyer, Emerson, was by my office today. Once again he began questioning my authority. He always entered my office without stopping at my secretary's desk and that was no fault of hers."

Boyler was not the least surprised by the journal entry as he had already experienced Emerson's rudeness and no real respect for anyone's title or place in society. But that did not bother Boyler. What did concern Boyler was Stevord's additional journal entry:

"Emerson always manages to get any prominent case that occurred in this county. He always managed to win at all costs. The one case though that staked out his reputation was when he defended a man named Paul Pipford. Pipford was accused of murdering a young couple. Their bodies were found in a crevice at the summit of Wright Peak. Emerson slyly had his client acquitted. I know Pipford was guilty but Emerson found an incredible way to find his client innocent of all charges. I know Pipford committed those murders. But the jury unanimously found Paul Pipford innocent. And within hours of his acquittal, Paul Pipford left the area.Today, though, he was particularly rude as he insisted on looking at the Hamilton family files."

Boyler knew the journal entries would provide him with many insights. And as Boyler had informed Chief Winston, it would take some time for him to sort through Alex Stevord's records, whether they were informal or formal documentations.

In addition, Stevord's description seemed to be rather detailed with great accuracy. This particular entry continued to state,

"*I am glad we had not digitalized our files yet as then I would have had no way of delaying his request. Emerson is a bully. No two ways about it. But I also know the Hamilton family papers will provide him with background he would love to get his hands on. There are descriptive papers about the Hamilton's financial resources and these are none of Emerson's business. I will do everything in my power to deter Emerson. Whoever the next coroner is will have to be aware of Emerson. I know the next coroner will not be a relative of mine as I am the last of the Stevords.*"

Boyler knew Emerson would be a tough character to deal with but he already realized the same could hold true with the Hamilton family and the body of Matthew Hamilton. The mayor had told him this would be a very complex job. Mayor Galente cautioned him on Emerson's so called prominence with the residents of Keene and surrounding areas. In so many words, Galente tried to alert Boyler of Emerson's intervention and intimidation. Now it was time to get to work and respond to Emerson.

"I know who you are. I appreciate your introduction. As you know already, there is a missing body."

Emerson looked at Boyler and realized he was no pushover.

"So, are you saying Matthew Hamilton's body has been misplaced?!"

"I cannot comment at this time."

Emerson stepped toward Boyler. Boyler stood his ground.Boyler did not really think Emerson would harm him physically. But he knew he was still testing the situation. What if Emerson did decide to hit him?

"Young man, do you know who I am?"

"Yes."

"I expect a response."

James Boyler looked at Sydney Emerson and repeated himself,

"I cannot comment at this time."

Emerson stared back at Boyler. Boyler was five foot ten inches and weighed 160 pounds. Yet Boyler was not intimidated by this rather large individual. Emerson continued to stare down Boyler. Then Emerson turned and left the coroner's office.

Emerson was used to getting his own way. And the new coroner, Boyler, could sense that immediately.

JAMES BOYLER

"Keep calm and carry on."

James Boyler is the sixth of six children. He was born in his parent's house in Saranac Lake and lived there his entire life. His father was a funeral home owner. His father also had the task of embalming the bodies transported to the home. As time went along James was shown the intricacies of the business. As no surprise to his mother, James took a great interest in learning every funeral home business facet of the funeral home establishment.

As his father explained to James, "The dead will keep us in business. Death is a part of life. We will always be above water with staying in business."

James' father died suddenly at the age of sixty. He was in a horrific car crash. Naturally the family turned to James to keep the funeral home in business. He was the only one of the Boyler children who had both the experience and training to run the establishment. His mother was glad that the funeral home would continue to thrive.

After doing so for three years, at the age of thirty three James was asked by a county representative to attend a special meeting in Elizabethtown to discuss the possibilities of who could be selected as the next county coroner as the most recent coroner who had served quite a long tenure had passed away.

Little did James know, until he arrived for the meeting, that he was the one and only individual the county board was considering for the position. Due to his experience with preparing and embalming cadavers along with assisting with autopsies as called upon, James seemed to be the natural candidate to select for the county coroner vacancy.

After consulting with his mother, siblings and his father's brother, who happened to be his godfather, James accepted the position. His uncle and one of his brothers assured James they could run the family funeral home with his guidance and assistance.

James was welcomed as a breath of fresh air by the county office employees. The county coroner's secretary was overjoyed as she had tired during the past few years of picking up the pieces of the prior coroner, Alex Stevord. Immediately the secretary could observe how organized James Boyler was and how he treated each person as a professional. He also reiterated the necessity to follow proper protocol. Little did he realize at first how often that was not followed by his predecessor. He quickly found out that he had his work cut out for him.

CHAPTER TWENTY*THREE

DIAL MOUNTAIN IS OFTEN CLIMBED WITH NIPPLETOP MOUNTAIN…

Emerson walked to his car, got in and sped away. He was going to drive to the police station in Keene and meet with Police Chief Winston. He did not have an appointment to see Winston but he planned to meet with him regardless. Again the snow was falling, even though the temperature showed thirty-five degrees on Emerson' dashboard. Emerson looked off to the right side of the highway and could see Hurricane Mountain rather clearly. The snow was not sticking to the roads. This was the warmest it had been in quite a few weeks.

Hurricane Mountain was one of the more difficult trails for hikers to climb. But it was still a popular rocky summit frequented by many. Hurricane Mountain offers one of the most spectacular views of any of the lesser peaks. It was not a forty-sixer but to many it felt like one of the high peaks. The elevation of the mountain is 3,694 feet.

Emerson arrived at the police station about fifteen minutes after departing the coroner's office in Elizabethtown. As he exited his car, his cheeks were rather red, more than likely from his high blood pressure and not the weather. Emerson's physician had constantly been warning him to lose weight and to monitor his diet. Emerson was known to eat an enormous amount of food no matter what meal he was partaking in. He walked up the walkway leading to the small police station. As he entered, Miss Landers, the police department secretary called out, "Mr. Emerson has arrived."

This did not surprise Emerson as he figured the coroner would call Police Chief Winston. Emerson knew he needed to keep his temper in check. He did not want to seem like he was a mad man. The Chief came out of his office and led Emerson back into it.

The Chief sat down and asked Emerson to do so too. He did not do so. Emerson was sweating profusely. Police Chief Winston was somewhat concerned that Emerson might collapse or even have a heart attack right there in the office.

“How can I help you?”

“You know exactly why I am here.”

Winston again asked Emerson to be seated. Emerson continued to pace around the office and spoke rather loudly. Miss Landers got up from her chair and quietly closed the police chief’s office door.

“What is going on with the status of Matthew Hamilton’s body? I am entitled to know as this is pertinent to Sean Metcalf’s defense!”

“Please sit down Mr. Emerson and I will provide you with more details.”

Emerson removed his coat along with his scarf and finally sat down across from the police chief. His breathing was rather heavy and he continued to perspire.

“We are in the process of sifting through the prior coroner, Alex Stevord’s file on the death of Matthew Hamilton. As soon as that task is completed, I will contact you.”

“How long will this process take to complete?”

“Today is Thursday so I figure by Monday afternoon. I have your telephone number so I will call you as soon as possible.”

Emerson picked himself up, put on his overcoat, snatched open the office door and departed without saying another word. Miss Landers immediately came into the office.

“Chief, are you okay?

"Oh, yes, it's just Emerson acting in his usual bullish manner. But this time he looks awful. I was afraid he might pass out or hyperventilate. I know this may sound odd, but he does not seem to be his usual self."

Miss Landers just looked at her boss, asked if needed anything else and then returned to her desk. She could only hope that Sydney Emerson did not return any time soon. In her eyes he was a belligerent man.

CHAPTER TWENTY*FOUR

SEWARD MOUNTAIN WAS NAMED AFTER ABRAHAM LINCOLN'S SECRETARY OF STATE, WILLIAM HENRY SEWARD, GOVERNOR OF NEW YORK STATE...

Sean was sleeping at his father's house that afternoon when his father heard a car come up the driveway. He was in his old bedroom, wrapped in a quilt his grandmother had made. It kept him quite warm, especially in this cold weather. His grandmother had been known to put together very creative and well sewn quilts. Sean thought she should have sold her pieces of work as the quilts were always admired by anyone who saw them.

Rita, Sean's mother, called out lowly to her husband Ryan in a concerned voice,

"Someone is here. Please get to the door before the person knocks. Sean is upstairs sleeping."

Ryan got up quickly from his desk. Even though it was his day off, he was working on reports. His career as a detective brought him numerous cases. Ryan never expected to be so busy with various cases of interest. He had a keen sense of investigating details of mysterious crimes. He had always wondered what had happened to his father. It was always an odd occurrence when his father disappeared; at the time Ryan was only five years old. His mother never really talked much about his father after he disappeared. He knew she became rather anxious whenever the subject was broached.

He had fallen behind with tending to his company's investigation reports as he was naturally consumed with Sean's plight. His supervisor understood and allowed Ryan whatever amount of time he needed with Sean to resolve the awful situation. Ryan's instincts told him that all would be resolved in Sean's favor.

He opened up the door to discover Sydney Emerson on the porch. Emerson was quite winded and agitated. Ryan was concerned with Emerson's physical appearance. Something was wrong with him. His breathing was rather rapid; Ryan was afraid Emerson might begin to hyperventilate.

"Please, come in."

Emerson stormed in, took off his overcoat and began to pace. If Sean could sleep through all the commotion stirred up by Emerson it would be a miracle. Ryan had never known Emerson to be as agitated as he exhibited at this moment.

Finally, after catching his breath, Emerson said,

"Something is wrong with this case."

"What do you mean?"

"Where's Sean?"

"He's upstairs sleeping in his bedroom. He fell asleep an hour ago."

Emerson continued to pace; his forehead was damp with sweat. He did not look well.

"Wake him up. I need to talk to him....alone...now."

Rita left the room and climbed up the stairs to check on Sean. If he was still sleeping she did not plan to waken him. She suddenly ran back down the stairs and into the living room.

"He's not upstairs! He's gone!"

The pressure of everything swirling around them was a strain on Rita, and Ryan as well. The whole situation was causing her to become rattled and anyone who even remotely knew her knew this was not her regular demeanor. And right now she looked exasperated.

CHAPTER TWENTY*FIVE

ROCKY PEAK RIDGE OFFERS OUTSTANDING VIEWS FROM ITS SUMMIT…

Ryan got up quickly and ran up the stairs to Sean's bedroom. Sean had numerous articles of clothing on the floor. His bed was disheveled and the room was cold. The window was partially open and Sean's coat was gone. Footprints in the snow led to the trail at the back of the house. Sean had often hiked that way when he was younger as he always liked the view at the top of the mountain behind the Metcalf house. It was always Sean's place of refuge. Ryan had found him there many a times. Sometimes Ryan used the place of refuge as well. It was a very peaceful place to go and sit and contemplate. Not many people were aware of its existence as the trail was in a remote place far away from any travelers or residents as well.

Sean put together the trail at an early age. From the time he started to walk Ryan would take him on different hiking excursions. Ryan was amazed at how fast and able Sean was with climbing the different trails he took him on. At the age of seven, Sean decided to blaze his own trail. Sean could see that there were different artifacts along the way in the woods. As a young boy, he researched the various items he found. Sean was convinced one or some of the various Iroquois Indians had frequented the trail.

Remarkably the trail Sean made was almost a mile long. The summit of the trail looked out on some of the forty sixers. On a clear day you could see Porter and Cascade Mountains. The view was beautiful. A few times, when Sean was a teenager, he camped out overnight alone at the summit. His mother never knew until later on that he did this. She would have been extremely nervous if she knew he had ventured and stayed overnight. His dad though always was told of Sean's plans.

There were times too, when Sean's mother, Rita would walk the trail, particularly with Ryan. As it did for both her son and husband, Rita always found the hike to be a peaceful walk.

Ryan ran outside and called out Sean's name. He knew the effort was futile as there was no response. But he knew he needed to continue to call out for Sean and if need be to go look for him. Ryan was exhausted. He hoped Sean would return as soon as possible. But he knew his son needed time to think things out.

Ryan came back into the house after calling out Sean's name a few times. He was even more concerned as the court had required Sean to remain at his parent's house and not leave the property, unless the judge approved a request. The trouble was manifested as Sean had a court-mandated bracelet around his ankle. It was possible that the local police station would receive a computer generated report of Sean's violation of probation. But Ryan was not overly concerned with that matter. He was concerned about Sean's safety.

Ryan turned to Emerson and was ready to ask him a series of questions. By this time Emerson had decided to sit down instead of pacing the room. Emerson looked as if he was going to pass out.

Emerson said to Ryan, "I really need to speak with Sean. But since he has disappeared, I will tell you and your wife. Sit down. This will take quite a while to explain."

So before Ryan could ask any questions, Emerson began to talk about the latest developments.

"I know he has not told you everything. But for starters, his fingerprints were identified on the inside of Matthew Hamilton's coffin."

"What?!"

Rita began to sob out loud. Ryan placed his arm around her. He asked Emerson to explain.

"I'm sorry; I should have told the two of you about the empty coffin."

Ryan and Rita looked at one another; they both were exhausted by the entire ordeal. The strain could been seen on both of their faces.

Emerson got up again from his chair and began to pace around the room. Ryan stood up and tried to catch Emerson's eye. Instead he said, "I do not understand."

Emerson was being somewhat reticent. Ryan felt as if he was holding back pertinent details about the situation. Ryan, for the first time, was having his doubts about Emerson being his son's legal counsel. Something just was not making sense. What bothered him was that he could not get a handle on what was happening. Ryan was becoming agitated as he always has had the distinct savviness to figure out complicated criminal cases, but now that his son was the individual being accused of something rather preposterous, Ryan was unable to put the pieces of the puzzle together. He found himself wanting to contact Anna Hamilton immediately. But this was not the time to do so.

SEAN METCALF

"Through life's trials we become better people."

Sean Metcalf was an only child. After his mother had delivered him, the doctors warned both Ryan and Rita that it could be life threatening if she was to bear another child. Ryan thought this would devastate Rita. But quite the contrary as she was so happy they had a child. Even more so, the baby was a boy so the Metcalf name would carry on. Upon hearing they should not have any more children their next immediate concern was the health of the newborn, Sean.

Sean weighed ten pounds and two ounces. It was quite an ordeal for Rita to deliver as the baby was rather large. The doctor assured Rita that a regular delivery could take place. Rita wanted to experience a regular delivery and not have to opt for a cesarean section. Even though it was a painful delivery for Sean's mother, both the mother and baby were in good condition.

Sean grew up to be a strapping young man. By the time of his sixteenth birthday he was six foot three inches and weighed two hundred and ten pounds. He played three sports in high school and was the captain of each of his soccer, basketball and baseball teams. His teammates considered him to be a true leader. Many felt Sean could get an athletic scholarship to the college of his choice. But Sean was unsure if he really wanted to go to college. It was a discussion he continually had with his parents.

Upon meeting Sabrina he fell deeply in love. She treated Sean like a hero. He hoped he could always reciprocate. Sabrina would often mention to Sean the love her mother and father had for one another. One time Sean was curious as to how Sabrina had such great insights into her parents' fondness for one another. One day Sabrina told Sean about the love letters she discovered in the attic of her home. Her mother, Anna, had neatly kept a series of letters her father, Sid, had scribed. Sean was surprised when Sabrina decided to read one of them to him:

My Love,

I knew the first day I met you that I wanted to spend the rest of my life with you and no one else. Your beautiful eyes pierced through me with such amazement. I felt as if we were the only two people in the entire world.

There were no distractions. It was only you and I. I know it cannot always be like that but I know when we want to we can find that special moment and place together. You are an incredible lady. I want you to know that! I will always treasure you like no other person can. Nothing can ever come between us.

With All My Love,

Sid

Sabrina shared this particular letter with Sean on a warm summer day when they were out in a row boat on the lake by her house.

But he also knew Sabrina's stepfather, Matthew Hamilton, was not too fond of Sean. He believed Sean was not a sincere person. He felt as if Sean was not true to his relationship with his stepdaughter, Sabrina. This was ironic as any one that knew Matthew Hamilton realized what a swine he could be. Sean never encountered a person who spoke highly of Matthew. Sean found this to be offsetting. He wanted to protect both Sabrina and her mother. But he was concerned that Matthew had such a hold on Anna. Sean did not want Sabrina's mother to be hurt or manipulated for that matter. Surprisingly she seemed somewhat naïve.

Sean also became determined to assist her with finding out what really happened to both her dad, Sid, and her stepfather, Matthew. She was consumed with the mysterious circumstances of both their deaths. Sean found himself wanting to do anything possible to help Sabrina. His determination to solve things was an attribute his parents always admired in him. But they often were concerned that Sean could sometimes take on other people's responsibilities at such an extreme level that it could lead to trouble or possible conflicts.

CHAPTER TWENTY*SIX

GRAY PEAK IS THE TALLEST OF THE TRAILLESS HIGH PEAKS…

Sean ran along the trail. He knew the details of the terrain as he had hiked this trail hundreds of times. And because he was the primary designer of the trail, he knew it so well he could probably walk it blindfolded.

There was a side trail that led to the main road. This trail was not as frequently utilized but Sean was able to walk it without any obstacles. The Metcalf house was only a mile away from Sabrina's family home. As he arrived at the main road, he began to jog along the side of it. Surprisingly the shoulder of the road was clear of the snow and ice. He kept an eye out for any cars as he did not want to be found. A vehicle suddenly came around a bend. Sean was able to dodge behind a tree so he could be hidden. He waited a few minutes before he reappeared on the roadway. He listened carefully for another approaching vehicle. His father had always told him you could hear things better in the woods during the winter when the leaves were down from the trees. He did not hear any cars coming along the road so he continued his walk to the Hamilton house.

It started to snow again even though it felt too warm to do so. But that was perhaps why Sean was sweating due to coming down the hiking trail and running along the road. The sun could be seen somewhat behind thin clouds. Sean was not dressed that warmly but still was perspiring. He finally arrived at Sabrina's house.

Sean walked onto the front porch. He listened carefully but did not hear any noise coming from inside the house. The house seemed rather still. He could hear the rustling of an animal off in the woods. He knew how to detect the different sounds as he had been used to the noises of the woods from all his years venturing the area trails. But other than the noises coming from the woods, things were silent, almost in an eerie way.

He knocked but no one responded or came to the door.

"Hello," he shouted out.

He waited to hear something.

"Hello. Sabrina!"

He went around the back of the house where a carport was located. There were no vehicles to be seen. Both Sabrina's jeep and her mother's car were not on the property. He went back onto the front porch and began to pace back and forth. He was not sure what to do next. A car came up the snow covered gravel driveway. The vehicle looked familiar as he peered through the hard falling snow. Before he realized it, the driver sounded the horn of the car, stopped the vehicle and emerged. It was Sean's father. He was alone.

Sean just stood there as his father approached the front porch. Sean then stepped off the porch and his father hugged him. His father did not say anything. Sean could tell his dad was just relieved that his son was fine.

"Dad, no one is here."

Ryan looked at the house and did the same thing Sean had just done. Ryan walked to the back of the house and also noticed there were no vehicles to be seen.

"Sean, I know this sounds somewhat odd, but I am surprised both vehicles are not here. Sabrina's mother does not like to drive in these weather conditions."

CHAPTER TWENTY*SEVEN

WHITEFACE MOUNTAIN, ON A CLEAR DAY, ENCOMPASSES VIEWS OF VERMONT, MONTREAL AND NEW HAMPSHIRE...

Sydney Emerson decided to stay at the Metcalf's house and asked Rita if he could use the telephone to call some people. His first call was to the county coroner. After the coroner's secretary answered the phone, James Boyler, the coroner picked up the telephone.

"Hello. This is James Boyler."

"Yes, this is Sydney Emerson. I apologize for my abrupt departure."

"I understand. I am here to assist you. I am not the enemy. But I am limited due to confidentiality laws."

Emerson sighed somewhat but proceeded to speak.

"I realize that but my client is quite upset. Frankly, so am I. Can I meet with you tomorrow?"

"Sure, Mr. Emerson. How is ten o'clock tomorrow morning?"

"Fine. I will see you at ten."

Emerson hung up the phone and then called the Keene police chief. Emerson informed him of his appointment with the coroner. Emerson asked the police chief to be there as well. Winston was not too keen about being ordered by Emerson to be at a meeting, but the police chief realized Emerson's abruptness was not to be taken so hard.

Rita asked if Emerson needed anything and if he would like a cup of coffee. He nodded his head and then continued to make another phone call. Rita, too, was used to Emerson's rudeness. She had known him for a very long time. She did not intend to listen to Sydney making his telephone calls but he spoke very loudly so it was virtually impossible to not hear what he was saying. Rita was becoming concerned with who he was speaking to. Why would he call the coroner first? How could that possibly help out her son,

Sean, with his case? She was also surprised he contacted the police chief. Rita felt Emerson was rather abrupt with each of the people he was talking to.

Emerson called Sean's cell phone. Sean answered it on the third ring. Emerson did not really expect Sean to answer. Sean was standing with his father in front of the Hamilton's house. Sean knew who was calling as his phone identified any incoming calls. He knew he had to answer this call.

"Hello Mr. Emerson."

"Where are you?"

"I am with my father."

"Can I speak to him?"

"I'll get him. Give me a moment."

Sean covered up the receiver and told his father Mr. Emerson is on the telephone and wants to speak to him. Sean's father took the cell phone from Sean and did not say much other than,

"Okay.

"Yes.

"I'll see you tomorrow morning at ten o'clock."

Ryan told Sean that Mr. Emerson asked for the two of them to be at the coroner's office tomorrow morning at ten o'clock. His mother could come as well, but Sean and his father knew she would be too nervous to do so. Sean asked why they were going to such a meeting but his father did not say too much. Of all places to convene why would they be going to the coroner's office? Sean also could not completely comprehend why his father seemed very reluctant to discuss his phone conversation he just had with Mr. Emerson.

Sean knew, though, that he had to stay as his parent's house. He knew the police could re-arrest him since he departed his parent's premises without permission. He knew he had taken a chance when he ran out of the house and went onto the trail. He felt quite anxious, especially knowing he had not done anything wrong. The oddity of the whole ordeal is that Sean still had not been made aware by the authorities or even his own lawyer for that matter as to what evidence or proof was discovered to legitimize his arrest. He began to speculate as to why Mr. Emerson had not yet explained the parameters of the case. In Sean's viewpoint, something just wasn't making any sense.

Sean did not realize that his father as well was becoming both suspicious and agitated with the situation and Emerson as well. The criminal justice system was quite disturbing as it did not seem to follow the philosophy that a person is innocent until proven guilty. Sean felt his rights as a citizen were being discriminated.He needed Mr. Emerson to be more up front with him and his parents.

The court mandated ankle bracelet had become quite an annoyance too. He felt like a prisoner in his parent's house. The ankle bracelet monitored his every move. He felt like he had a surveillance camera attached to his body.

REVEREND METCALF

"You cannot rebuke the storms of life if there is a storm on the inside of you."

TEN YEARS AGO

The reverend had been able to keep his prior family separate from his current situation. His wife, Patricia, and their two daughters, Katherine and Kelly, knew nothing about Reverend Metcalf's first marriage and family. It had been quite some time since Reverend Metcalf was in Keene or any part of the Adirondacks. The reverend never officially filed any paperwork to declare his divorce or separation from his first wife. It would have made no sense to do so as he was officially declared dead seven years after he disappeared. Amazingly, to this point in time, his family did not have any inclination that he had fled from Keene so many years ago and left behind a shattered family. But he always feared someone would discover his whereabouts in Canada.

The reverend had been able to keep track of his two sons. He was aware his elder son Michael lived in Lake Placid. Even though his other son, Ryan, lived a short distance away in Keene, the two of them did not have frequent contact with one another. The reverend also knew his son Ryan, would often probe and inquire as to the possible finding of him. The reverend realized he needed to be savvy enough to keep abreast of his son, Ryan, and his investigative prowess. He knew his son had a stellar reputation for investigating and resolving complicated cases. Throughout the years he was able to keep track of his son's career and the various cases he was able to solve. It was easier to monitor all of the cases as the reverend utilized the internet to keep up to date on the latest happenings but he would only do so from computers not in his home. The city library was a good place to frequent as he was an unknown there. He limited his visits as he did not want to be known as a regular visitor to the establishment. He was always cautious due to his circumstances.

The reverend knew it would not be easy to outsmart the Metcalf family, especially his son. Ryan. The reverend realized it could be foolhardy to utilize the internet at home to keep tabs on the happenings in Keene as his wife is a computer technician and she could easily detect his usage of the computer websites and programs he would navigate to discover pertinent information.

The reverend also decided to tap into the services of an individual he knew was intelligent enough and quite frankly slick enough to provide him the information he would need to keep abreast of his family's daily routines, and more importantly the inquiries they would put forth to find him. The use of a prepaid cell phone was his communication mode. This way no one else would know he was making contact with his informant.

Reverend Metcalf dreaded that someone would find him but he knew the man to assist him would be worth the monies he would pay him. And that person was Sydney Emerson.

CHAPTER TWENTY*EIGHT

LOWER WOLFJAW MOUNTAIN HAS FIVE APPROACHES TO ITS SUMMIT…

When Ryan and Sean had returned to their house, Rita was at the door to greet them. She ran down the steps and gave Sean a long embracing hug. Tears were streaming down her cheeks. She was extremely happy Sean came back to the house. She was in somewhat of a panic, afraid the police would detain him again. But that was not the only reason she was releasing such emotion. She knew she had to speak to Ryan about her concerns with Sydney Emerson's telephone calls.

The three of them walked back into the house. The telephone was ringing. Rita truly hoped it was not Sydney Emerson calling. Ryan went over to it and picked it up.

"Hello."

"It's Sabrina." She hesitated a moment and then continued,

"May I speak to Sean?"

Sean's dad became agitated, which is a rarity for him to exhibit. As a detective he always portrays a calm and collected demeanor. He then said to Sabrina,

"What do you need to talk to my son about?'

"I just need to speak with him.'

Rita moved to Ryan's side. She had stopped crying but was shaking from the cold outside and her feelings of concern about Emerson. Sean was standing at the front door.

Ryan responded, "I do not think so. You can come over to the house instead."

Sabrina hung up the telephone without a response.

Sean came into the living room and asked who was on the telephone even though he already knew.

“It was Sabrina.”

He wondered why she was calling now.

Ryan then said, “She might be coming over to the house.”

Rita said, “Do you think that is such a good idea?”

On top of everything else on Rita’s mind now they had to concern themselves with Sabrina coming over to their house. She knew she could not discuss Emerson’s phone calls with her husband right this moment. She did not want to worry her son, Sean, with her thoughts and she would not discuss this matter in front of Sabrina either.

Sean did not say anything out loud but he thought to himself why now? What did she want to tell him? He sat down on the couch in the living room and stared at the fireplace. He knew his parents were being very tolerant and patient with Sabrina. His father knew that her life was not an easy situation. Her family had suffered so many different episodes, ones that Ryan could not really tell Rita and Sean about. Due to the nature of his investigations with his agency, he was privy to many of the happenings of Sabrina’s family. In addition, he was aware of many of the details of Anna Hamilton’s life.

Anna had expressed her trepidation to Ryan about Matthew Hamilton only a few weeks after she married Matthew. On a gloomy day, Anna happened to stop by the local luncheonette for a cup of tea and the establishment’s delicious pastries. Ryan happened to be seated at the counter. She sat down next to him and they shared some small talk. One thing led to another and Anna expressed to Ryan that Matthew was constantly delving into her finances and inquiring as to how she gained all her wealth. Anna further explained to Ryan that Matthew subtly hinted he had a friend who could better manage her monies. Anna suddenly stopped talking about her plight when of all people to enter the luncheonette was Matthew himself.

Anna never discussed this with Ryan again until it was necessary. Ryan could only speculate to himself who this person may be. He had a very good idea as to who it could be.

Sean and his parents sat down and awaited Sabrina's arrival. Each of them seemed too exhausted to even talk at this time.

SYDNEY EMERSON

"Patience is more worthy than miracle working."

Sydney Emerson was considered by many to be a pompous ass. But when things became difficult for a person, especially if it involved the law, Sydney was the first person anybody would turn too. Emerson probably did not have a true friend in this world. He exhibited such a mean streak at times, that not many ladies really took an interest in him, even though he is highly intelligent and believed to be rather wealthy.

Emerson always seemed to be, as people would say, "…at the right place at the right time." Some would say quietly that he reminded them of an ambulance chaser. He seemed to have a say in practically every single case that came up in the local courts.

Emerson would be so bold to take on any opponent. His record was quite impressive. His work ethic was better than anyone else's. He did not rely on any other lawyers or co-counselors to assist him with his cases. This was unusual for such a high profile lawyer. But then Emerson was not one of your ordinary, regular lawyers. Due to that reason alone, people expected nothing but the best when they contacted and hired Emerson to be their counsel. He would devote one hundred percent effort to a client's case no matter how big or small.

The people of Keene never really knew too much about Sydney Emerson's private life. He was known to not ever really reveal anything about his personal life. He never had any children and as far as it was known he married once but his wife left him. People speculated as to why she departed but no real news could be found out and that was unusual for Keene to experience.

Emerson was a true workaholic and he was known also as an individual whom enjoyed eating. His physician continually warned about his weight. Many would say Emerson was obese. As many people were aware, his bulk was rather imposing. His physician would often warn him that his fast paced lifestyle of dealing with so many different legal cases could have an adverse effect on his health. But Emerson continued to shake his head in an affirmative manner without ever heeding the doctor's advice. Emerson was quite an obstinate man but his physician knew it was his duty to monitor Emerson's health plight.

Emerson amassed quite an amount of money. He not only charged outrageous fees for his services but he also invested in many different areas. Emerson was able to rely on a prominent Lake Champlain realtor who always seemed to be ahead of the curve on any type of real estate availability. Emerson was known to take phone calls right in the middle of legal procedures. Even though the judge would become perturbed, Emerson would continue with the call as it was always from the realtor.

Emerson practically owned most of the commercial buildings in Keene, Keene Valley, Elizabethtown and parts of Lake Placid. He had a stranglehold on the real estate market. The local realtors despised having to work with Emerson on any type of real estate venture. He seemed to be quite cut throat with whoever and whatever dealing he had. Sometimes he would leave some of the realtors, especially females, in tears as his harsh approach would cause such angst. His clients, at times, would be embarrassed by his behavior. But remarkably no one would put him in his place as he always seemed to get whatever he wanted. This would sometimes occur with all sorts of shenanigans. People would sometimes wonder, as well, if his dealings were always legal. But again no one questioned him or reported some of his controversial decisions to the proper authorities.

Ironically, he met his wife during one of these real estate meetings. He seemed skeptical at first with her interest in him, but once he researched who she was and discovered she was quite wealthy he let his guard down. In unusual fashion, he rained many gifts of admiration upon her. When she reached her fiftieth birthday, he gave her a fully paid car. He celebrated their first anniversary by booking a two night stay at a reclusive cabin in Saranac Lake. When they went their separate ways, years later, she did not seek to gain any of his wealth. He heard from her on his birthday and Christmas day. Other than that he did not have any contact with her. Strangely, at times, he did miss her though.

Upon her departure Emerson became an even more mean spirited person. And that was quite a feat in itself. He always seemed to be out to get anybody who stood in his way. And he wasn't about to let that occur.

CHAPTER TWENTY*NINE

ARMSTRONG MOUNTAIN IS NAMED AFTER THOMAS ARMSTRONG, A 19TH CENTURY LUMBERJACK…

Sabrina arrived within fifteen minutes after she had hung up the telephone. Ryan opened up the door and Sabrina came into the house. He could tell she had been crying. She looked rather disheveled. She was not wearing any makeup and her hair was pulled back in a pony tail. Sabrina was not dressed warmly either. Her overcoat looked more like spring apparel.

"Please sit down. I will go upstairs and get Sean."

"No need to, Dad, I'm right here."

Sean emerged from the hallway. He remained standing. He did not wait for Sabrina to start speaking.

As his mother came into the living room, Sean said,

"Sabrina, my parents found out that I knew about the empty coffin."

Sabrina looked up at Sean. The she said,

"I knew that. But I need to tell you something else."

Sabrina glanced over at Sean's parents. They were both seated on the couch by the fireplace. Then she looked back over at Sean. She seemed to hesitate to say anything. It seemed as if she did not want to speak to Sean about her concern with Sean's parents in the room. But she realized Sean would not have it any other way. She realized how close Sean really was to his parents even though he had little or no contract with them during the last few months.

She quietly uttered, "I believe my stepfather is alive."

****

Sean's parents looked quite confused. Yet when they looked over to Sean, he was not at all taken back by Sabrina's news.

"Sean, I'm sorry I had you check my stepfather's coffin. I know the police are aware your fingerprints showed up inside his coffin."

She hesitated. She turned to Sean's parents.

"I believe he is alive. I keep receiving phone calls from a private number. But each time I answer the person does not speak. There is a period of silence where I know someone is on the other end."

Sabrina was having a very difficult time expressing herself. She started to cry but then was able to continue.

"Except the last time the person called, I said hello twice and the person said, "'I love you, precious.'"

Sabrina began to sob uncontrollably.

Sean glanced over at his parents. He went over to comfort Sabrina while his mother went into the kitchen to get a glass of water for Sabrina. Sabrina was able to calm down somewhat and spoke some more. As Rita returned to the room Sabrina continued.

"Even though I hated it only my stepfather has ever called me that. No one except my mother knew he called me precious….no one." She began to shake and cry again.

Sean's father walked over to the living room window and gazed out at the mountains. This view always seemed to give him the opportunity to clear his mind and sort out his thoughts. If it wasn't for such a chaotic situation, he would normally go for a walk with his wife to get some fresh air and much needed exercise. He was both anxious and stunned at the same time. He knew, too, this could only be good news for Sean. But he was still uneasy with the whole situation. So many things were not making sense. His innate ability to resolve a case seemed to elude him. And this he found to be discouraging.

CHAPTER THIRTY

SEYMOUR MOUNTAIN IS PART OF THE SEWARD RANGE...

As Ryan knew rather well, news would once again travel fast through Keene. The murder of Matthew Hamilton, or possibly the missing Matthew Hamilton, was on everybody's mind. People were becoming both restless and angry. Many were feeling angry as they felt they had been fooled by the Hamilton family. The residents of Keene had rallied around Anna Hamilton after the now supposed drowning of her husband, Matthew Hamilton. But to now hear he is alive, they felt somewhat betrayed.People actually began to ponder if Anna knew all about Matthew Hamilton's faked death.

Ryan called Sydney Emerson on the telephone and asked him to come over to the house. He needed to speak to Emerson in a candid and possibly stern manner to find out more information. He knew Emerson could be somewhat belligerent.

Emerson said, "We're meeting tomorrow morning at ten o'clock. Can't this wait until then?"

Ryan simply said, "No."

"Why?"

Ryan was getting agitated.

"Please come to our house. I do not want to talk over the phone."

Emerson was annoyed as well but then said,

"Fine. I'll be over in half an hour."

Emerson did not enjoy being told what to do. But in this case he abided in Ryan Metcalf's wishes. Emerson realized it could be worth his while.

Sabrina was now sipping from a steaming cup of tea that Sean's mother had prepared.

"Have you told your mother about the telephone call?" asked Sean's father.

"No."

She sipped her tea slowly as if to avoid answering Ryan. She did respond though.

"I did not want to alarm my mother, especially if the calls were unreliable and possibly a hoax. The last call occurred earlier today so I knew I had to tell Sean right away.'

It was already over forty-five minutes since Sydney Emerson said he would arrive at the Metcalf house. It was very unusual for Emerson to be late for anything. The roads were all clear of snow and ice. The highway department had been utilizing liquid deicer to combat the roadways. It worked wonders.

A flashing light could be seen coming up the driveway. Ryan opened the front door and as he did so, a police car was approaching the house. There was only one officer in the car. Ryan wondered why the officer was utilizing a flashing light. The policeman got out of the vehicle, kept the flashing light on, put on his hat and walked toward the front porch.

MARK WINSTON

"Let peace be our quest and our aim."

Mark Winston had become a member of the Keene police department right after he graduated from the Upstate Police Academy. He finished first in his class with honors. He had excelled in all areas of the police training program. When he was hired as a police officer in the village of Keene, many thought he would be stationed here for a very short period of time. But that was for naught as he and his family became fixtures of the area. Later on he was promoted to the role of police chief. He appreciated the new title but his job did not really change much.

When he first became a police officer in Keene he was hired as a full time officer and there was a part time officer as well. The part time officer owned the local bakery shop. When Mark became the police chief there were three other officers on the staff. The population had not changed much in the past three decades but there seemed to be more issues the officers had to be involved with in the village. Some of the newcomers did not seem as invested in the community as did the longtime residents. This was a change Mark felt bad about. Keene had always been a close knit group of people.

Sometimes though Mark would become bored and restless with his role as the police chief. He truly loved the area he resided in with his family but there was nothing out of the ordinary for him to be challenged with, other than an occasional fight by teens in the village or at the local school or perhaps a drunken brawl at the local tavern. Other than that he led a quiet and efficient police department. And that was true until the odd case of Matthew Hamilton came to the forefront. There were other cases to deal with but this one took on a life of itself.

Mark knew he might be ill prepared to handle the depth of the case before him. He was a proud man, one who did not really rely on other people's advice or input. His colleagues would often comment that he was too good for the role of police chief he had assumed. But this case presented him with quite a challenge with bizarre twists and turns.

CHAPTER THIRTY*ONE

NIPPLETOP IS OFTEN CLIMBED WITH DIAL MOUNTAIN…

The police officer did not look familiar as there were only four policemen employed by the local police station. He was not an officer from the Keene police department as Ryan knew each and every one of them. He looked similar in appearance to the police chief, Mark Winston. But his demeanor was somewhat rude and abrasive, unlike MarkWinston's welcoming way about him. All the officer said when Ryan opened the door, without identifying himself, was,

"You are Mr. Metcalf?"

Before Ryan could even respond the officer said,

"Your son, Sean, is to come with me, now."

Rita appeared behind her husband and said,

"Why? And who are you?"

"Hello madam. Your son needs to come with me."

Rita shook her head back and forth. The officer began to step into the house even though the Metcalfs did not ask him to do so. Nor did Ryan or Rita make way at the doorway so the police officer could enter, especially since they did not who this mysterious and unidentified police officer could be.

Ryan went to grab the officer's arm, but then thought differently. Something just wasn't right with this scene especially without the officer identifying himself. But Ryan was concerned as to what was transpiring before their eyes in such quick fashion. What recourse did they have with this police officer? Who was he?

Ryan instead stated,

"Do you have identification so we know who you are and what jurisdiction you represent?"

Suddenly there was a loud crash from the back of the house. The officer ran outside to the back of the house. He did not see anything. It was difficult to maneuver quickly as the ground was covered with over a foot of snow. Sean suddenly appeared out in the front yard.

Sean just stood there and yelled out to his mother and father,

"Call Mr. Emerson! Find out where he is and tell him to meet me at the diner."

"What's going on?"

But Sean had already gotten into his dad's SUV and left. The officer reappeared from the back yard. He looked over to Sean's parents and did not say anything. He got into the police car and left as well. He was right behind Sean.

Ryan immediately ran to the telephone to put a call into Emerson. But before doing so he called Police Chief Winston to inform him of the appearance of the unknown police officer. The phone rang four times before it was answered. Winston immediately spoke into the phone before Ryan could utter a word.

"Ryan, I know why you are calling. Please come down to the police station. Is Sean with you?"

Ryan just hung up the telephone without responding to the police chief. Ryan did not even get the opportunity to ask the police chief who the unidentified police officer could be. He turned to Rita and told her he was going down to the police station. Rita said she would stay at the house in case Sean returned. Rita's last words to her husband were for him to drive carefully. He kissed his wife goodbye and walked over to his wife's SUV. But before he got into the vehicle, Rita had called out to Ryan and told him she was going to come with him. She knew it would be too difficult waiting at the house alone.She grabbed her coat and purse and got into the SUV. They quickly travelled down the road.

CHAPTER THIRTY*TWO

UPPER WOLFJAW MOUNTAIN HAS ONE VERY STEEP PORTION…

Emerson was already waiting in a back booth as Sean pulled up alongside the diner. It was beginning to snow again but hardly anyone seemed to notice. As a regular routine, the snowplows were out tending to the roads. It was a regular occurrence for the area. Emerson was being served a hot cup of steaming coffee as Sean entered the diner. This eating establishment was known for its delicious coffee and homemade pies, especially the blueberry pies.

Sean looked exhausted. He had on a blue hooded sweatshirt, jeans, hiking boots and a baseball hat. He spotted Emerson and sat across from him in the booth. Sean had not shaven in a couple of days and his eyes were rather bloodshot. He looked as though he could use twenty four hours of sleep.

Emerson just glanced at Sean with a sullen look. He knew Sean was about to tell him something important. Was it about Sabrina? Or perhaps Mr. Hamilton? Maybe both. Emerson asked the waitress to come back over to the booth so Sean could order something to eat. Sean was quiet and did not look at Emerson. He did though ask the waitress for a cup of coffee and a bowl of soup.

"Chicken noodle?"

"Yes, thank you."

She nodded, smiled and headed toward the kitchen to get his order.

"Where have you been?"

Sean did not answer at first. He sighed and then took off his hooded sweatshirt. Underneath he was wearing a blue t-shirt. The waitress returned with the cup of coffee and a large bowl of chicken noodle soup. The soup was a house specialty.

Finally Sean spoke; Emerson was not a patient man.

“I know I have been confusing you Mr. Emerson. But I’ll explain why.”

Emerson nodded and awaited Sean’s explanation. Typically he was not a man to await anything. But this time he knew things were different. At first Sean was not surprised by Emerson’s level of patience. Emerson did not want to appear over anxious and barrage Sean with a series of questions. Sean wondered why Emerson was being so calm about everything. It just was not his way.

HIM

"Embrace adversity before it embraces you."

It was quite easy to subterfuge a person's bank records. In this day and age of sophisticated technology so many people were mesmerized by the swiftness of the immediate access to one's finances. But for HIM, it was a great challenge to swindle people's investments.

He had a great sense of how to break into a person's account without ever being detected. He always did this in the privacy of his home. He was a loner so he often could accomplish these tasks without interruption. He enjoyed the challenge of beating the system. He never was unsuccessful with gaining access to a person's bank accounts. He was trusted by the people of the community and no one would ever suspected HIM.

Little did any of his victims know, he dwelt in the midst all of them. His biggest challenge was swindling from the richest known widow in Keene. Mrs. Anna Hamilton did not monitor her accounts. She relied on her daughter, Sabrina, to do so. When Anna married Matthew Hamilton, he knew he had an inside connection to all of Anna Hamilton's financial records. He was absolutely delighted.

He relied heavily on Matthew Hamilton's ability to swoon Anna to fall in love with Matthew. He was able to quickly gain Anna's interest. But the reality was that Matthew Hamilton expected to become rather wealthy by marrying her. In addition, he would channel some of her funds to HIM. He was diabolical with his scheme. Matthew was almost fearful of not following along with his plan. And this was not the only time he would plot along with HIM.

He was also mysterious with some of his cases. He also would come in contact with people involved in bizarre life circumstances. Those people would contact HIM and ask for the most complex services he could provide legally. Naturally he would charge them great legal fees knowing they could not and often would not seek someone else's assistance. Again, being a longtime resident of the area enabled him to play this treasured role.

<u>CHAPTER THIRTY*THREE</u>

TABLETOP MOUNTAIN IS ONE OF THE TRAILLESS HIGH PEAKS...

Sean was rather fatigued but the cup of coffee, and especially the bowl of chicken noodle soup, seemed to invigorate him. The last few hours had caused him much distress and anxiety. He was reminded of a prayer his grandmother would always recite:

"God is our refuge and strength, a very present help in trouble." (Psalm 46:1)

This excerpt came from the Book of Psalms. Sean was quite familiar with the Psalms as his grandmother would often refer to them, especially if a person needed to reaffirm his or her faith. His grandmother was a very religious person. She was not overzealous with her faith but Sean knew she followed in the footsteps of Jesus. Sean often sought her guidance particularly when things became troublesome for himself.

Emerson looked at Sean and awaited his promised explanation. Sean took another sip of the coffee. He decided to drink it black. He was purposely delaying his conversation with his lawyer. He was feeling a bit uncomfortable. Sean put down his mug and looked at Emerson.

"I do not know how to begin but I'll do my best."

"Go on," Emerson said, not in a demanding manner but in a soothing way instead. The waitress walked by their booth but decided not to bother them as she noticed Sean and Mr. Emerson were engaged in a rather serious looking conversation.

As Sean began to speak, he recognized the police vehicle turning into the diner parking lot. It was the same one that had been at the Metcalf's home a little while ago. But this did not seem to distract Sean. Even though the officer had not identified himself at the house, he was not his immediate concern. Sean figured there had to be some sort of reasonable explanation about the mysterious officer. Someone had to know who he was.

"I know I need to tell you what has been happening. My fingerprints are inside Mr. Hamilton's coffin. But for reasons you cannot even imagine, I know where…"

Suddenly a loud commotion took place at the entrance of the diner. Two police officers, along with Police Chief Winston entered noisily into the diner. They quickly spotted Sean and came over to the booth Emerson and Sean were at. Sean looked agitated but was not in a panic.

Chief Winston directed his comments to Sean. The police chief seemed a little agitated with Emerson. He did not give Emerson any type of a warm greeting.

"You have violated your house arrest conditions. You are to come with me."

Sean looked over at the other two officers and recognized one of them as the police officer who was at his parent's house. Sean knew he was not a Keene police officer but yet could not figure out what his involvement was with this case. Sean was going to inquire but realized this was not really the time to do so.

Emerson asked for a moment to talk to Sean. Police Chief Winston hesitated but then allowed Emerson and Sean to have a couple of minutes. Winston walked away from the booth.

Emerson spoke to Sean in a very quiet voice.

"Sean, did you remove Matthew Hamilton's body from the coffin?"

"Yes…and no."

"What?!"

“It sounds bizarre but Sabrina does not believe it was her stepfather, Matthew Hamilton’s body.”

“I do not understand.”

Sean was afraid Police Chief Winston would walk back to the booth before he could give Emerson all of the details.

He continued,

“Sabrina is frightened to come forward as she fears Matthew Hamilton.”

“But I thought he was dead.”

“He is alive.”

Emerson looked at Sean but then glanced away as he said,

“Then who was in the coffin?”

“Sid Messier. Somebody must have switched the bodies. But then later on took that body out of the coffin.”

Emerson tried to keep his voice to a murmur when he said, “Who?”

Winston began to walk over to the booth. Emerson stood up and requested another minute to complete his conversation with Sean. Winston, without saying a word, reluctantly nodded his head in the affirmative, backed up a few steps and turned back to the diner counter where he had been seated. Emerson sat back in the booth.

Before Sean responded he looked at Emerson carefully as he thought Emerson knew every person in Keene. Sean then responded,

“Sid Messier is Mrs. Hamilton’s first husband.”

"So where is Matthew Hamilton? And I thought the coffin was empty when it was opened at the coroner's office."

"I am not sure but Sabrina believes she has been getting telephone calls from Matthew Hamilton. The caller does not speak. But his last call he finally said something."

"When?"

"The last few days. He has been calling every night."

"Why?"

Sean thought Emerson's inquiries were kind of odd but Sean continued to answer them. Sean was somewhat concerned that Emerson was asking so many questions.

"Sabrina said..."

"What, Sean? Why is Matthew Hamilton making contact now?"

Emerson was visibly upset. This confused Sean even more so as Emerson never seemed to get startled by anything.

Sean realized he had to tell Mr. Emerson now, before Police Chief Winston walked back over to the booth.

Sean then uttered, "Sabrina said Matthew Hamilton killed Sid Messier. He murdered her father."

CHAPTER THIRTY*FOUR

MOUNT COLDEN IS KNOWN TO BE A POPULAR PEAK FOR HIKERS…

Emerson looked at Sean and said,

"So, Alexander Stevord, the longtime coroner, knew all about this! And I'll bet Anna Hamilton does too. But now the question is why."

Sean looked at Emerson in a forlorn manner. He was confused by Emerson's proclamation. Sean was not so naïve to know Emerson had not let him and his parents become privy to additional information.

Why was Emerson asking so many questions? Sean began to wonder if Emerson had Sean's best interests at heart. Why did he become so uncomfortable with the latest information? Perhaps he was covering something up. And who was this mysterious officer who not only was previously at his house but now appeared at the diner with Police Chief Winston.

Sean urgently wanted to get home and see his father. He needed to ask him so many questions. He also wanted to express to him his concerns about Mr. Emerson. And he needed to be in the comfort of his parents and their home. Their home was a safe haven.

The Police Chief had waited long enough. His patience was long but now he walked over to the booth. Sean got up from the booth, asked Mr. Emerson to call Sean's parents and inform them he was going to the police station with Chief Winston. Emerson followed behind them to the police station in his own vehicle. The unidentified officer did likewise.

CHAPTER THIRTY*FIVE

SAWTEETH HAS ONE OF THE BEST VIEWS IN THE ADIRONDACKS PARK…

Sean's parents were at the police station when Chief Winston, the two officers and Sean had arrived. Sabrina was also there but she was sitting in her car in the parking lot. Sean's parents were not aware she was there.

Sean exited the police car. He was cuffed and escorted by the two officers. Sean was becoming rather agitated as he knew this scene was uncalled for, especially since he did not murder Matthew Hamilton. He also did not understand who the unidentified police officer was who came to his parent's house and was now escorting him into the police station.

Police Chief Winston walked over to Sean's parents. Sean's mother and father were seated inside the waiting area of the police station. They were asked by Winston to come into his office. They slowly got up from the bench and followed behind the police chief.

Sean's mother, Rita, was sobbing as Sean's father, Ryan, put an arm around her. Chief Winston asked them to be seated as he walked around to his desk and sat down before him. Everything on the police chief's desk was orderly. The police chief was known to be an extremely organized individual. His attention to detail was well known and appreciated.

"I know you are waiting for an explanation. So I will tell you what I know at this time."

Sean's parents held hands, remained quiet and looked quite distraught.

"Matthew Hamilton is alive and we believe he is armed. He killed Sid Messier, Anna Hamilton's first husband."

Ryan Metcalf began to say something, but thought wiser and sat back in his chair and waited for the police chief to provide further details. But Chief Winston hesitated, so instead Ryan asked,

"What does this have to do with Sean? Why is he being detained?"

"Because we believe he…"

"Chief! Sean Metcalf has gotten away! He left through the side door exit!" a startled police officer reported excitedly to Chief Winston. This was the officer Sean could not identify. He seemed shaken by the sudden change of events but he remained calm and heeded the police chief's advice and direction.

Winston quickly got out from behind his desk and said, "What? When?"

"Just a few minutes ago. We left him in the holding cell for more questioning and when we returned a few minutes later, he was gone!"

The Chief asked, "Was he still handcuffed?"

The officer looked down at the floor and mumbled, "No, he wasn't."

Rita's wailing was earth shattering. She began to scream and fell into Ryan's arms.

Ryan said, "What is going on? Mark, who is the unidentified officer? You obviously brought him on to help investigate the situation."

Chief Winston could only look at Ryan; he did not respond.

"What is our son being held for? Why did you handcuff him again and bring him here. Chief Winston we want some answers!"

Again, oddly, Winston did not respond.

Ryan's father added, "And where is Sydney Emerson?"

The police chief realized he owed Rita and Ryan Metcalf an explanation. Ryan wanted answers now.

RITA METCALF

"Discipline is knowing what you are doing and doing it the best you can."

Rita Metcalf, a very distant cousin of Anna Hamilton, found herself to be happily married to Ryan Metcalf. Ryan brought about a semblance of order to their lives. When they first met she thought Ryan was an arrogant man. He did not seem to have a warm personality. But when he asked her out to dinner she readily accepted. He took her to an Italian restaurant in Plattsburgh. The restaurant looked old from the outside but upon entering the establishment her opinion of the place and Ryan's taste for a great place for a first date was outstanding.

The meal was absolutely delicious. They sat for almost three and a half hours enjoying their culinary choices and their conversation. There was no lull in their talking whatsoever. They found so many things to talk about. Rita found herself even telling Ryan that she was not the least bit impressed when she first met him. But that was at a local carnival and Ryan seemed to be preoccupied. She later found out that was because one of his cousins had just passed away.

Rita shared with him some of the doings of her family. He could tell she adored her cousin Anna and how she seemed to be concerned with her life and the decisions she made. Rita told Ryan that sometimes Anna would make decisions without thinking with any sense of logic.

Rita was amazed how much she shared with Ryan on their first date. As they departed the restaurant, he opened the passenger door for her. Upon arriving at her family's house he simply asked her if he could give her a kiss good night. She quickly responded affirmatively. He did so and then she got out of the car. Ryan walked her to the front door and she went inside.

Her mother was seated in the side room and asked Rita if she felt she would have another date with Ryan. She smiled and simply said to her mother, "Yes."

But there was always Rita's concern for her cousin Anna. Anna was a well to do lady due to Sid's more than able care of her. He waited on her cousin hand and foot. People of Keene would often comment to Rita about what a gentleman Sid was to not only Anna but to anyone he came in contact with. But Rita's biggest concern was when Sid died and the scoundrel Matthew Hamilton came into the picture and tried to sweep Anna off her feet. He seemed to be two faced but Anna was oblivious to Matthew's manipulation and persuasion. Rita knew better!

CHAPTER THIRTY*SIX

DIX IS OFTEN CLIMBED BY HIKERS BY ITSELF…

Sean sat in the jail cell. The odor in the cell was awful but Sean got used to it. His hair was disheveled, as were his clothes. He desperately needed a shower but it did not seem as if that would be provided. He desperately wanted to get out of here.

An officer came by to check on Sean and to see if he was sleeping. Sean looked up at the officer and did not say a word, especially since the officer was the one who did not identify himself to Sean and his parents.

The officer looked over at Sean and said,

"The judge will be here in a half hour. Your parents have not arrived yet."

Sean looked up again, but he said nothing. The officer departed. Sean wondered who this officer could be. It seemed odd that he still had not formally identified himself. But he had to be someone Police Chief Winston had hired or why else would he be there. It was not something though that Sean spent much time thinking about. His more immediate concern was to get out of this jail cell. He was beginning to become claustrophobic.

He found himself speculating as to what was going on. He felt Sabrina or her mother could not possibly have anything to do with Matthew Hamilton fabricating his death. Yet Sean was still being detained for something he did not do and for an incident that did not really happen, especially since it was known that Matthew Hamilton was alive. He needed to be released.

The police officer reappeared. He opened Sean's cell and took the handcuffs off of Sean's wrists. The officer told Sean to go down the hallway to Chief Winston's office.

Sean asked, "Without you?"

"Yes."

Sean was quietly elated. He kept looking over his shoulder thinking this was a trap or set up of some sort. But it wasn’t.

SYDNEY EMERSON & PAUL PIPFORD

"You can suffer anything if you believe in yourself."

Sydney Emerson had never had any interest in Paul Pipford's hiking adventures. Even if Emerson wanted to go hiking, he would be unable to do so due to his immense weight and high blood pressure. Nor was Emerson the least bit interested in Pipford's shop. He was curious though about this young man's instant popularity upon his arrival to Keene Valley. He was mystified by his lack of connection to anyone in the area even though he heard Pipford had climbed all forty six of the High Peaks. Pipford seemed to be a loner even though his shop and booked hiking excursions were rather successful.

Ironically, Paul Pipford was the man who made Sydney Emerson into a rather prominent lawyer. Many said that without Paul Pipford, Sydney Emerson's career and reputation would have never skyrocketed. To local folks, Emerson was known as a cutthroat counselor of the law. He seemed to win every petty case. But he never seemed to be involved in complicated felony situations until the arrest of Paul Pipford for two homicides. Pipford contacted Emerson immediately.

During the Labor Weekend, Paul Pipford had scheduled an overnight hiking excursion to Wright Peak, named after Governor Silas Wright. The venture would also include two other high peaks. Included in this excursion were ten individuals including Paul Pipford. Three people from northern Vermont had contacted Pipford in June requesting reservations for the Saturday to Sunday Labor Day Weekend extravaganza. Four college students from Paul Smith's College had signed up for the overnight hike. And a newly married couple from New York City had contacted Pipford the first week in August inquiring about a Labor Day Weekend hiking trip. The nine hikers were instructed by Pipford to meet him at the Adirondack Loj.

The group ascended the mountain and settled down near the summit. They staked out small areas to eat their lunch.

The group members readied themselves to journey on the next part of the hike. Margaret and Jonathan Smithson decided not to leave with the group. The group, with Pipford's advice, departed without the Smithsons. The party of seven spent the day hiking the two other trails and descended the mountains and arrived back at the Adirondack Loj at seven thirty in the evening. They all went their separate ways and returned in the morning for an additional hiking excursion.

Three weeks later Paul Pipford was informed that two bodies were discovered at the summit of Wright Peak in the crevices of where the B-47 bomber had crashed in 1962. Due to the cooler temperatures at the summit, the bodies stayed pretty well preserved. A week later Pipford was arrested and charged with the murders of Margaret and Jonathan Smithson.

The defense of Paul Pipford was the case Sydney Emerson was awaiting. He knew he could now exhibit his legal talents. But he never expected the case to become so sensationalized by the press. He loved this factor as it would give great exposure and have potential clients flocking to him.Yet he always seemed to stay one step in front of both the media and the district attorney assigned to prosecute the case. He prided himself on being able to do this. He would not allow anyone to beat him.

The people of Keene and Keene Valley along with the surrounding area were mesmerized by the murders of Margaret and Jonathan Smithson. Not much was initially known about the Smithsons, as the young couple was not from the area. It was soon discovered though that they were from Westchester County. Other than some basic and mundane events of the day, there was not really any other highlighted news that interested the public.

Paul Pipford on the other hand was a mystery man. Even though he was quickly welcomed by the small Adirondacks community he became an anomaly. Emerson knew he could sway a jury to find Pipford innocent of the homicide charges. He knew there just was not enough credible evidence to tie Pipford to the crimes he was accused of doing.

The people of Keene and the surrounding area realized the double homicide trial of Paul Pipford would be mesmerizing. The trial itself would take place at the county seat in Elizabethtown. The court room would not be able to accommodate all of the people expected to attend but there was no other alternative unless the trial was moved downstate to Albany. But that did not seem likely.

CHAPTER THIRTY*SEVEN

PHELPS MOUNTAIN BORDERS MOUNT MARCY AND MARCY DAM…

Matthew Hamilton approached the village of Keene with great apprehension. He knew he stirred up quite a commotion by disappearing, especially after his body was exhumed and his body was not found in the coffin. He was able to retrieve a newspaper from a garbage receptacle at the local deli. The headline simply read:

"HAMILTON ALIVE!"

Hamilton's picture was published alongside the newspaper headline. He did not resemble the man in the photograph. He took a few moments to read the article:

The residents of Keene wake up today with remarkable news. Matthew Hamilton, the second husband of Anna Hamilton, has mysteriously returned to the community. Matthew Hamilton had been declared dead less than two years ago. Many people of Keene had attended his funeral service.

The sudden reemergence of Hamilton has sent this town and the surrounding areas into a tailspin. Mayor Galente has asked the townspeople to remain calm as the investigation team led by Police Chief Mark Winston have put forth an all-out effort to find Matthew Hamilton.

The realization that Matthew Hamilton is alive would now place a new perspective on the arrest of Mr. Sean Metcalf for the homicide charge of Matthew Hamilton. As has been confirmed by some witness accounts, Matthew Hamilton is alive. Thus this would duly relieve Sean Metcalf of any murder charges.

The town of Keene has a history of enduring odd criminal cases. Many could recall readily the bizarre case of the young married couple and their bodies being discovered on top of Wright Peak. The suspect, Paul Pipford, was found innocent. To this day many people of this region feel Pipford was guilty of the horrific crime.

Old timers most definitely could remember the gory death of a wife by the hands of her husband. She was a physically disabled woman who was accused by her husband of having an affair. The husband became so enraged he decapitated his wife, placed her head on a backyard picnic table, and then commenced his chore of chopping wood.

More details will be emerging as to what really happened with MatthewHamilton, his fabricated death and his appearance back in Keene.

Matthew Hamilton found himself breathing rapidly as he finished reading the news article. He knew he needed to set the record straight. Who was going to believe him?

Though he was bundled up in a winter coat, he had lost twenty five to thirty pounds since the time of his planned disappearance. Was he willing to allow the lead suspect, Sean Metcalf, to be arraigned and possibly indicted on murder charges? He knew that would not be the thing to allow happen but at this point in time he knew if he was apprehended he would have a lot of explaining to do. He knew he was not going to do so by himself. He knew whohe had to get in contact with and he realized this had to done as soon as possible.

Suddenly a car came down the main road. Hamilton stepped back into the woods so he could not be discovered. He walked back onto the trail leading to Anna Hamilton's house. Could this be a safe haven? He thought why not as it was the place he used to reside at. He wanted to approach his wife, Anna, but he did not want things to become more complicated than what they were already. He would not be surprised if she turned him away. He knew too that this sudden change of events would surely take a toll on her. He meant no harm to Anna or anyone else. But he knew people would mistrust anything he might say unless he could prove he was set up.

CHAPTER THIRTY*EIGHT

SADDLEBACK MOUNTAIN HAS OUTSTANDING VIEWS…

Once again the snow was falling at a strong pace. Some of the High Peaks trails were closed down due to treacherous conditions. But that never seemed to deter some of the expert hikers of the region venturing onto the trails and sometimes spending a few nights in the mountains. This became a major worry for the rangers as a rescue of lost hikers could be life threatening for the rescuers. Sometimes the weather conditions could change drastically and possibly become a whiteout. The hikers and the rescuers could all be lost.

Anna Hamilton was in her living room with a hot cup of tea. She was so stressed out by the situation. She had been informed by Chief Winston of the latest news. Was her second husband, Matthew, alive? Did he commit a murder? Why did he disappear?

Anna now realized why Sabrina always seemed somewhat distant with Matthew. Sabrina always seemed to have an insight to things that Anna could get a grasp on. Sabrina never really trusted Matthew. She was continually questioning his day to day routine and doings. He always seemed to be sneaky with any dealings with Anna's monies. Sometimes Anna would inquire as to what was occurring with her investments. Matthew always tried to reassure there was nothing to be concerned about.

The whole situation about Matthew had become a living nightmare. So many people were upset by the ordeal. The news that had transpired was not making any sense to so many of them.

Sabrina, Anna's daughter, had left the house to go the jail to see if she could speak with Sean. Chief Winston gave Sabrina approval to come to the jail but he did not know when she could see Sean. Anna looked out the window. The view of the High Peaks was spectacular but that did not seem to put her at ease as it had usually done for her inthe past. She felt rather lonely. Neither the cup of tea nor the comfort of her home could relieve her anxiety.

****

Matthew Hamilton had made his way along the trail even though it was snow covered and visibility was poor. As he came upon the house he could see her looking out the large bay window. Should he approach the house? Would his appearance startle Anna? A pickup truck ascended the hill. Matthew was not sure who was in the vehicle. He could see two people in the pickup truck. Was Sabrina driving? Was that Sean Metcalf with her? Any time Matthew thought about Sean he became quite uneasy. Matthew knew that Sabrina was aware of Matthew's feelings and that made Sabrina angry. She often wished her dad, Sid, was still alive. Matthew eased himself back onto the trail and crouched down.

The overhead light of the grey pickup truck illuminated the interior of the vehicle. Matthew was somewhat surprised to see both Sabrina and Sean emerge. Sabrina was crying and Sean had his arm around Sabrina's waist. The front door of the house opened and Anna came out onto the porch. Matthew could see, even from a distance, how old she appeared to be. Matthew felt she looked haggard and distraught. He could also hear their conversation.

"Please hurry up and come inside."

"Why are you so worried?" Sabrina asked her mother. Sabrina tried to curtail her tears but was unable to do so.

"Hurry up. It is too risky to be outside."

"Okay. We're coming."

Sean hesitated for a moment and looked around as he thought he heard something. His years of living in these parts had trained him to identify the different types of noises in the woods. Sean could sense that something was not right. He was going to walk toward the woods but he knew that would upset both Sabrina and her mother. He then looked at Sabrina and her mother and the three of them went inside the house and closed the door. Matthew reemerged from the woods but did not approach the house. Matthew thought to himself that he must locate the man who could help him out. Or rightfully change things for the better.

REVEREND EMERSON

"Strengthen us in our daily crosses."

PRESENT DAY

During the last few weeks Reverend Metcalf had become somewhat paranoid. His wife, Patricia, commented a few times on his jumpiness. One weekend they were at a remote rural area. They had decided to utilize a friend's cabin that was located on the shore of a scenic lake. The back drop reminded him of the High Peaks he knew of so long ago when he resided in the Adirondacks.

But the weekend was abruptly interrupted early Sunday morning when his contact phoned him to let him know a colleague of his son Ryan was making his way to the cabin as he was able to track down their whereabouts by a fluke citing while he was vacationing in the area. This unnerved Reverend Metcalf. His wife was quite baffled by the sudden change in plans.

CHAPTER THIRTY*NINE

SOUTH DIX WAS RENAMED CARSON PEAK FOR RUSSELL M.L. CARSON, PAST PRESIDENT OF THE ADIRONDACK MOUNTAIN CLUB…

Anna, Sabrina and Sean quickly came into the house. Anna began to weep. Just a moment ago she seemed as if she was in control of her emotions. Now she was glad Sabrina had come back to the house. She was also both happy and confused as to why Sean had arrived.

"Please tell me what is going on."

Sean looked over at Sabrina waiting for her to respond to her mom's inquiry. Sabrina remained silent for a few moments, walked across the room and gave her mother a hug. Anna felt as if she had become the child and Sabrina was acting as the mother figure. Anna though seemed to find this comforting to her. She knew she was having a very difficult time with understanding what was happening with Matthew. She felt so many different emotions. On one hand she felt anger. How could he let us all go through the ordeal of burying him and grieving afterwards? On the other hand she felt a real sense of betrayal. Why would he fake his death and then disappear all together. She also felt ashamed as so many residents of Keene had showed her such great compassion and support upon the death of Matthew. Anna was dealing with all of these thoughts and emotions as Sabrina was hugging and consoling her.

Sabrina then released herself from the hug and said, "Mom. I know Matthew is alive. And I know he is somewhere in Keene."

Softly she continued, "Why didn't you tell me?"

A knock was heard at the front door. Anna looked startled. Even though Sabrina was home Anna was rather stressed out. The ordeal had aged her in the past few days. Sabrina, too, became frightened as she thought the person on the front porch could be Matthew Hamilton. Neither Sabrina nor Anna went to open the door. The person knocked a second time. Sean looked over to both women. Sean approached the door, hesitated to open it, but did say,

"Who is there?"

At first, there was no answer. Sabrina peeked out the front window and the turned around and exclaimed,

"Sean, it's your mother!"

Sean quickly opened the door. His mother was covered with snow and was shaking. Sean and Sabrina brought her inside, removed her coat and sat her down. It was rare for Sean's mother to drive, nonetheless in this horrific weather. Rita always had either Ryan or Sean drive her whenever she had to travel someplace. She often would walk to town when the weather was nice. Just the fact that she drove to the Hamilton's house would bear some importance. No one had yet said anything.

After what seemed like an immense amount of time, Sean's mother spoke.

"Sean, there won't be any charges filed against you."

She was shivering. Anna handed her a cup of hot chocolate. Anna figured it would warm her up and provide her with some nourishment and comfort. Rita did not thank Anna for her kindness. This seemed somewhat odd for his mother to not show any appreciation.

Sean then said, "Where's Dad?"

As Rita took the cup of hot chocolate from Anna she seemed somewhat perturbed.

She then looked at Anna and said, "Did you know Matt was alive? Did you?"

Sean and Sabrina were baffled by Sean's mother's sudden change of mood. She had become accusatory toward Sabrina's mother. Anna hesitated to respond to Rita's questioning concerns.

Sean again asked,

"Mom, where's Dad?"

But Rita did not respond to Sean's inquiry. Sean began to wonder why his mother came to the Hamilton's house. All he could see was his mother's anger toward Anna Hamilton. Perhaps the stress of the whole situation was bearing down upon his mother.

Sean raised his voice to his mother and repeated, "Where is Dad?"

He then said, "What are you not telling us!"

PART FIVE

TRIAL OF PAUL PIPFORD

The trial of Paul Pipford on the double homicide of Margaret and Jonathan Smithson brought more prominence to Sydney Emerson than anyone could have ever predicted. There were not too many lawyers in the county who could possibly take on a case of such a formidable level. Even though Emerson had been involved in numerous lower level cases, he was so sure of himself that he knew he could take on Paul Pipford's murder trial, do the investigation and gain a victory for the defense of Pipford. He had no doubt whatsoever or at least that is what he wanted everyone to believe.

Emerson was given six weeks to prepare for the trial. It seemed like a very short period of time. Even though Emerson requested an extension of time knowing the judge would deny him, he was sure enough he could prepare for this case of a lifetime with the allotted six weeks. Remarkably, he relied on his own investigative skills to ready his client and prepare. He did not and would not rely on anyone else. Anyone who really understood Sydney Emerson, knew Emerson trusted no one else except himself. But could he really do all the leg work needed to present a defense for Paul Pipford. Time would tell.

TRIAL: DAY ONE

"All rise. The Honorable Joseph Anderson is the judge for the case of Paul Pipford."

The judge made his way to his chair. His desk was elevated above the crowd. And what a crowd it was. The court room was packed. There was no air conditioning as the room was cooled with six ceiling fans. Obviously the room was very warm on this July afternoon. There would be concerns that some people could experience heat exhaustion.

The judge read the charges of double homicide to the jury. He explained that in order to find Paul Pipford guilty of the charges they must find no reasonable doubt. He went on to explain what he meant. The twelve jurors nodded their heads affirming their understanding of the charges and what the expectations were to find the defendant guilty. Surprisingly these twelve jury members were selected the week before in quick fashion.

Before asking the respective lawyers if they were ready to present opening arguments, he asked the two court clerks to clear the courtroom of anyone not seated. This was met with some grumbling as close to sixty people were escorted outside the courtroom and to the lawn area. This location was crowded with over three hundred people both sitting and standing. They were ready to listen to the trial which would be broadcast over loud speakers which had been installed to accommodate the overflow of the crowd. It was quite an amazing scene!

The judge then asked the prosecutor, who was the district attorney of Essex County, if he was ready to proceed.

"Yes, your honor, I am ready."

"Please proceed."

THE PROSECUTION: OPENING STATEMENTS

The prosecutor slowly got up from his chair and walked over to the jury. He could see most of them were sweating already and it was only nine thirty in the morning.

"Ladies and gentlemen, I will keep this short and sweet. Paul Pipford has no alibi. He took a group on a hike to the summit of Wright Peak with the intent to murder a well-to-do couple. Margaret and Jonathan Smithson trusted Paul Pipford with their lives. He delayed their descent from the summit while he sent the rest of the group down the trail. He gave them both a poisonous bottle of water. Within minutes they both sat down, passed out, and then Pipford placed their bodies in the crevice where an aircraft had crashed in 1962. He plotted their deaths. No one else is to blame."

Margaret Smithson's mother could be heard sobbing. Margaret's father had died two months after her daughter and son-in-law were murdered. Jonathan Smithson's parents sat stoically holding hands, showing no emotion.

The judge then proceeded by asking the defense lawyer, Sydney Emerson, to present hisopening statements.

THE DEFENSE: OPENING STATEMENTS

Sydney Emerson could be a very intimidating individual. He got up from his seat in a rather quick manner especially for a man of his immense size. He looked at his client, Paul Pipford, then practically leered at the jury. He was known to utilize any advantage with any case he was responsible for regardless of how small or large. This case was huge and everyone knew it.

"Realize it from the onset, Paul Pipford is innocent. He led a group to the summit of Wright Peak. He was with the group on both the ascent and descent of the mountain. Margaret and Jonathan Smithson were both careless and naïve. They both decided to drink the water from the running stream on the way up the mountain. They both stayed behind at the summit when Paul Pipford instructed them to descend the mountain with him. The Smithsons, clear and simple, took ill at the summit, moved themselves to the crevice of the mountain, fell asleep, and died from the poisonous water. There is no other explanation. I will prove my client's innocence."

Emerson again looked over at his client, PaulPipford, with a sympathetic face. He then stared back at the juror box as he swayed his head from side to side. Emerson then walked over to the defense table and dropped his large body onto the chair next to his client.

The judge then said,

"I know it sounds odd but I am postponing the presentation of witnesses for tomorrow as I have just been made aware by the court clerk that our air conditioner system is working in reverse and the heating system has activated itself and is not shutting off. With that said, I am sequestering the jury overnight to an unspecified hotel. The jury is to proceed to my chambers. Mr. Pipford is to be escorted out of the court with his lawyer as Mr. Pipford is out on bail. Thank you."

The court clerk then announced,

“Please stand as Honorable Judge Anderson is now leaving the bench.”

THAT NIGHT

This sudden hold on the trial of Paul Pipford allowed time for the attendees to speculate on so many levels. At the local luncheonette people could be heard murmuring all sorts of questions.

"Where has the jury been taken?

"Why is Pipford out on bail while the trial has just started?

"When did the poisonous water hypothesis become a possibility?"

"I never read about that in the newspaper!"

"Why is Sydney Emerson so confident?

"I heard the Smithsons planned this as a double suicide."

And the people's theories and ideas were left up to debate all day long as they hoped the trial would commence the next day.

THE NEXT DAY

The next morning the sky was crystal clear. Overnight the heat wave had broken. Surprisingly the temperature at seven o'clock registered at forty eight degrees. The hope was that the heating and air conditioner system had been fixed. An announcement would be made by eight that morning with the possible resumption of the trial scheduled for nine thirty. At eight ten a sign was posted at the front door of the courtroom announcing a ten o'clock commencement of the trial

The local radio station along with the internet news agencies announced the trial's continuation. By nine o'clock the court room was once again standing room only. The people standing hoped the judge would allow them to remain in the courtroom.

JUDGE ANDERSON

Judge Anderson knew how to control a court. Before he entered his courtroom he had duly instructed the court personnel to escort the standees from the courtroom. In addition, he instructed there to be no people seated in the first row respectively behind the prosecution and defense tables. This was a somewhat different arrangement but Judge Anderson wanted a tightly controlled court room.

The weather was cooperating and that was a relief. In addition, the heating and air conditioner system had been fixed. The local repairman was a guru. He had the system repaired and ready to operate in less than thirty minutes.

Judge Anderson was extremely pleased to see how organized the courtroom appeared when he entered it at exactly ten o'clock. He believed in running an orderly courtroom. He knew practically each and every one of the jurors by name. That came with his longtime tenure of forty years on the bench. He knew his community and the residents well. There was though one jury member he had never seen before. That jury member had an almost permanent smile on his face. Anderson thought to himself, he would find out more about who he is.

THE JURY

The jury was selected in quick fashion. Even though each member of the jury knew details of the Paul Pipford case, they were each selected by the defense and prosecution because they felt they each would be impartial and able to listen to and assess all of the evidence and information to be presented.

The jury was quite a mixture of personalities and that seemed a little unusual for a community of this size.

Juror One: Male; Caucasian; 56 years old; lifelong resident; retiree;widower; three adult children, all residing in the area.

Juror Two: Female; Caucasian; 24 years old; waitress; single; resides with mother; father deceased.

Juror Three: Male; African American; 32 years old; forest ranger; married; two children; wife in hospital for long term cancer care.

Juror Four: Male; Hispanic; 29 years old; unemployed; single; parents own luncheonette in Elizabethtown.

Juror Five: Female; Caucasian; 20 years old; nursery worker; single; relative of Police Chief Winston.

Juror Six: Male; Caucasian; 42 years old; two year resident; teacher; married; five children; wife: secretary for Lake Placid Chamber of Commerce.

Juror Seven: Female; Asian; 51 years old; Keene Stewart's Shoppe Assistant Manager; divorced; no children.

Juror Eight: Male; Caucasian: 82 years old; retiree; one time mayor of Saranac Lake; married for 64 years; three children, one deceased: killed by a hit and run driver.

Juror Nine: Female; Caucasian; 68 years old; Elzabethtown Funeral Home employee; married; husband assists at funeral home; no children.

Juror Ten: Female; African American; 36 years old; married; Keene Central School District Board of Education Vice President; four children; husband: Lake Placid shop owner.

Juror Eleven: Male; Caucasian; 26 years old; single; divorced once; one child: lives with grandparents in Tupper Lake; miniature golf co-owner; filed for bankruptcy six weeks ago.

Juror Twelve: Female; Caucasian; 90 years old; widow for thirty-seven years; wealthy; owner of successful online clothing retail shop; served on twelve prior juries in Essex County.

The jury consisted of six males and six females. The breakdown was unusual for the Adirondack region. Usually a jury would be dominated by males. Yet Sydney Emerson and the prosecutor came to quick consensus on the jury. Emerson was pleased even more so when juror one was selected as the foreman. Emerson knew the juror for over ten years.

PROSECUTION WITNESS #1

"Are you ready to present your witnesses?"

"Yes, your honor."

"How many do you have?

"Four, your honor. Perhaps a fifth."

"Objection," shouted Sydney Emerson.

Judge Anderson then asked the prosecutor to clarify.

"Your honor, we have a witness who has not arrived yet in the courtroom.'

"I will decide on the witness' validity if need be. As of now the witness has not been approved as you listed four prosecution witnesses on the docket. The objection, Mr. Emerson, is sustained for now.

"Please proceed."

The prosecutor went over to his desk, shuffled some papers and then called Claire Blake to the witness stand. After she was sworn in, the prosecutor proceeded.

"Ms. Blake, please state your full name to the court."

"Claire Marie Blake.

"Age?"

"I am twenty two years old."

"What is your occupation?"

"I am studying to be a nurse."

"Did you ever pay for the services of a hiking tour guide for a hike to Wright Peak?"

"Yes."

"When, Ms. Blake, did you do so?"

"This past Labor Day Weekend."

"Did you go alone on this hike?

"No."

"Who else went?"

"Two of my friends from Vermont. We planned this hike last spring."

"Who did you contact?"

"Paul Pipford."

"Is he in this courtroom?"

"Yes. He is seated at the defense table."

"Ms. Blake, could you tell me how comfortable you were with Mr. Pipford as your hiking guide?"

"At first I had no issues with him. But when we got ready to descend Wright Peak he became testy."

"With whom?"

"The Smithsons."

"Ms. Blake, are you referring to the deceased?"

"Yes."

"What did Mr. Pipford do?"

"He became rather impatient with the Smithsons. He was annoyed that they were not ready to go back down the mountain."

"Did he speak to them in a rude manner?"

"I would say so."

"Did the Smithsons come down the mountain with the group?"

"No."

"Did Paul Pipford descend with the group?"

"Not at first. Our group began to go down the mountain but he was not with us at first."

"Who is he you refer to?"

"Paul Pipford."

"When did he catch up to the group?"

"I would say about ten minutes after we started down the mountain."

"How did he seem to you?"

"He was out of breath."

"Your honor, I have no further questions for Ms. Blake."

The judge looked over to Sydney Emerson. He did not seem to be getting out of his seat to cross examine Ms. Blake.

"Mr. Emerson, do you wish to cross examine?"

"Yes, your honor,"

Emerson looked at Claire Blake but did not get up from his chair as he commenced his inquiries.

"Ms. Blake, was this your first hike?"

"Yes."

"Ms. Blake, would you consider Paul Pipford to be an experienced hiker?"

"Yes."

"Ms. Blake, did Mr. Pipford provide you and your group members bottles of water before you departed for your hike to the summit of Wright Peak?"

"Yes."

"Did you finish your water before reaching the stream?"

"Yes."

"Did the Smithsons do likewise?"

Before the prosecutor could object, Ms. Blake said, "Yes, I believe so."

The judge allowed the response into the record.

"Ms. Blake, was your breathing escalated as you descended the mountain?"

"Yes."

"So do you think it was abnormal for Mr. Pipford to breathing harder as he returned to your group?"

"Not necessarily."

"Your honor I have no further questions for this witness."

Judge Anderson then said, "Ms. Blake you may step down from the witness stand."

As Ms. Blake proceeded to do so the judge asked the prosecutor to call his next witness.

"I call police officer Mark Winston."

PROSECUTION WITNESS #2

Police officer Mark Winston made his way to the witness stand and then he was sworn in.

"Do you swear to tell the truth, the whole truth and nothing but the truth, so help you God?"

"I do."

As Officer Winston was about to testify he wondered as to why he was being called as a prosecution witness. About all he could provide was his presence on the summit of Wright Peak. He had been flown by helicopter to the summit upon the trail ranger's telephone call to the police station.

"Please state your full name to the court."

"Mark Bryant Winston."

"And your occupation, sir."

"I am a police officer with the Keene police department."

"Officer Winston, why were you asked to proceed to the summit of Wright Peak?"

"A group of hikers discovered two bodies in the crevice of the Wright Peak summit."

"How did they come upon the bodies?"

"One of the people was walking around where the remains of an airplane had been scattered due to an airplane crash in 1962."

"What did the person find?"

"As I stated previously, two bodies."

"What type of condition were they in?"

"The two bodies looked as if they were just sleeping there."

A muffled cry could be heard in the court room. It was Margaret Stevenson's mother trying to contain her emotions.

"Did you notice anything peculiar?"

"No. Other than the two people's bodies were side by side holding hands."

Again Margaret Stevenson's cries could be heard. It was mesmerizing.

"Officer Winston, was there any reason to believe these two people, Margaret and Jonathan Smithson died of natural causes?"

"No."

"Thank you Officer Winston. Your honor, I have no further questions for this witness."

Judge Anderson said, "Mr. Emerson, do you wish to cross examine the witness?"

"Yes, your honor. I will be brief. I only have a few questions for Officer Winston."

This time Emerson got right out of his seat and walked rather quickly to the witness stand. Surprisingly, for the physical size Emerson was, he was quite nimble on his feet. This even took Winston for a surprise.

"Officer Winston, would you consider yourself a thorough police officer?"

"Yes, sir."

"Did you know the Smithsons were drinking water from the stream along the trail on the way up to the descent of Wright Peak?"

"Yes."

"In your professional experience and your knowledge of the High Peaks region, is it advisable for anyone to drink the water from the area streams?"

"No."

"Thank you Officer Winston. Your honor, I have no further questions for this witness."

Emerson's last remark was rather snide. Most of the jury members noticed how cocky Emerson appeared as he returned to the defense table. As Emerson sat down, he seemed to have a smirk on his face.

PROSECUTION WITNESS #3

The judge seemed to be getting restless as each of the first two prosecution witnesses had no real substance to present to the jury to convince them that Paul Pipford had committed this awful double murder.

"Please present your next witness."

"We call Robert Sutter to the witness stand."

Mr. Sutter, who appeared to be no older than eighteen years old approached the witness stand. He was a strapping young man, weighing about two hundred and twenty five pounds. He looked as if he could take on the world.

"Please state your full name to the court."

"My name is Robert Justin Sutter."

"Are you employed?"

"No. sir, I am a student at Paul Smith's College."

"What are you majoring in at the college?"

"I am majoring in forestry and minoring in physical training."

The judge then said to the prosecutor. "Please pick up the pace of your questioning of this witness."

"Yes, your honor.

"Mr. Sutter, did you know the deceased couple?"

"No. I met them the day of our hike."

"Do you know the defendant Paul Pipford?"

"Yes. This was the third time I hiked with him."

"Did you see Mr. Pipford exhibit any hostility toward the Smithsons?"

"Yes, just before we departed the summit."

"Does Mr. Pipford appear to be a physically fit individual?"

"Yes."

"How would you know that?"

"Mr. Pipford seemed to hike at a good pace. In addition, my education as a physical trainer has prepared me to notice who is physically fit."

"Do you believe Mr. Pipford would have the strength to lift a person weighing one hundred and twenty pounds?"

"Yes."

"How about a person weighing one hundred and eighty pounds?"

"Objection," Emerson said.

"On what grounds Mr. Emerson?"

"Mere speculation, your honor."

"Overruled. I will allow the witness to answer the question."

"Yes."

"I have no further questions for Mr. Sutter."

Before Judge Anderson could ask Mr. Emerson if he wanted to cross examine Mr. Sutter, Emerson had already proceeded to the witness stand.

"Good morning Mr. Sutter. You seem to be in good physical shape Mr. Sutter."

"Thank you sir."

"Could you lift a body weighing one hundred and eighty pounds?"

"Yes sir," Sutter stated with a sense of pride.

"What about two hundred pounds?

"Most definitely."

"Did you proceed down with the rest of the group as you departed the Wright Peak summit?"

"Not initially. I was concerned with the manner Mr. Pipford was speaking to the Smithsons."

"What did you do?"

"I walked over to Mr. Pipford and asked him to come down the mountain."

"What did he say?"

"I am right behind you. Don't wait for me."

"And did he do what he said?"

"Yes. He came up behind me within a few minutes."

"Was Mr. Pipford breathing heavily?"

"No. No more than any of us."

"Were the Smithsons with you?

"No. They decided to stay behind."

"How do you know that?"

"I heard Mr. Smithson tell Mr. Pipford to go ahead."

"I have no further questions your honor."

“Mr. Sutter, you may step down.

“So, any further witnesses?’ the judge said wearily.

“Yes, your honor. We call Alexander Stevord.”

PROSECUTION WITNESS #4

The witness made his way from the back of the courtroom. Most people in the courtroom knew of this witness. He was the well known coroner of the county. No one ever really questioned his findings or better yet his credentials.

"Sir, please state your full name to the court."

"Why of course. I am Alexander Lincoln Stevord." He looked as though he was going to wave to the spectators in the courtroom. But he did think not to do so.

"Please tell the court your occupation."

"Well naturally you know me as the county coroner. And I am proud of it!"

"Please tell the court your involvement with murders of Margaret and Jonathan Smithson."

"Yes, well I was required to examine the bodies of Mr. And Mrs. Smithson. I completed autopsies on both of them."

"Mr. Stevord, could you tell the court your findings?"

"Yes. As Officer Winston stated earlier the bodies of Margaret and Jonathan Smithson appeared to be in a sleep like state."

Emerson knew the coroner would try to personalize the deceased couple by using their names. But Emerson knew it would be to no avail as he was convinced he could win this case.

Stevord continued with his testimony, "But as I have stated in my report I discovered lacerations to the back of Margaret Smithson's head and a scrap to the right side of Jonathan Smithson's cheek. This would align to my findings that each of them had endured some type of injury."

The prosecutor looked over to the jury members; each of them showed little or no emotion. The prosecutor realized he needed to tie the Smithson's injuries to the defendant, Paul Pipford.

"Mr. Stevord, do you believe these injuries were caused by another individual?"

"Yes."

"Do you know who could have done this?"

"Well, I believe it had to be a male. No offense meant, but the injuries to Margaret Smithson were brutal and I do not believe a female could have done that type of harm."

"Thank you sir. I have no further questions for Mr. Stevord."

"Mr. Emerson, your witness." It was almost without question that Emerson would cross examine Mr. Stevord. The judge felt it was not necessary to ask Mr. Emerson if he wanted to question the witness.

Mr. Emerson did not get up from his seat. Instead he made his inquiries without getting up.

"Good day Mr. Stevord. Did you conduct the autopsies alone?"

"Yes sir."

"Do you always conduct the autopsies alone?"

"No sir."

"Why were these done by yourself?"

“Well…I felt it was too big of a case to bring in someone else.”

“Of course, why shouldn’t you with such a sensational case.”

“Objection!” shouted the prosecutor.

“Sustained,” said Judge Anderson, “You know better than that, Mr. Emerson. You know you are not allowed to make editorial comments during the questioning of witnesses. The jury will disregard Mr. Emerson’s comment.”

But Emerson knew the jury members would not automatically erase the comment from their minds. His ploy would be effective.

“I apologize your honor. Mr. Stevord, are you good at what you do as a coroner?”

“Yes sir.”

“Do you film the autopsies you perform?”

“Yes sir.”

“Were you drinking during the autopsies of the Smithsons?”

“No sir.”

“Your honor, I would like to submit as evidence the videotape clips of the Smithson autopsies. The videotape is three hours in length but I would ask if the jury could view the excerpt at the 22:35 mark of the tape. At this juncture the jury will be able to clearly observe Mr. Stevord drinking beer. This continues for awhile as he consumes at least five bottles of beer during the next forty minutes of the autopsy.”

Judge Anderson sighed slightly and then said, "I will allow the videotape to be viewed."

Surprisingly the prosecutor did not object. As the jury watched the videotape, Mr. Stevord remained seated on the witness stand. When the approximate forty minute video clip was completed, Emerson continued his cross examination of Mr. Stevord.

"Mr. Stevord do you need a glass of water?"

"No. No thank you." Mr. Stevord was sweating quite a bit.

"Mr. Stevord, I will ask you again, were you drinking during the time you performed the autopsies of Margaret and Jonathan Smithson?"

"Yes. I was drinking."

"Were you drunk?"

"I am not sure."

"Do you have proof that Paul Pipford committed the alleged murders of Margaret and Jonathan Smithson?"

Stevord sheepishly said, "No sir, I do not."

"Mr. Stevord, thank you for your time," said Emerson.

"Mr. Stevord, you may step down from the witness stand," the judge embarrassingly stated.

As Mr. Emerson turned to his client, Mr. Stevord made his way out of the courtroom. Stevord knew he had not aided the prosecutor well. The judge then looked at the jury for a moment before he spoke.

"Ladies and gentlemen, you have endured quite a bit today. I am ending our session for today and will reconvene tomorrow at nine thirty in the morning. Again the jury will be sequestered for the evening."

And with that the judge got up, the clerk asked for everyone to rise and the judge departed the courtroom.

THAT AFTERNOON

There was rarely a crowd at the luncheonette at three in the afternoon. But today was not your usual day. Quite a crowd gathered there upon leaving the courtroom. The talk of the various people was quite consistent.

"What is the prosecutor doing?"

"Why isn't he presenting a more solid case?"

"Those poor parents. They looked devastated."

"I think they believe the case is hopeless."

"How could Pipford be found guilty?"

There was not an empty seat at the luncheonette. Everyone was rather loud. But the luncheonette owner did not mind whatsoever. Business was booming. Selfishly, he could only hope the trial would go on for quite a few more days. But that did not seem to be what would occur.

DAY THREE

The trial was delayed for forty five minutes as Sydney Emerson and the prosecutor met with Judge Anderson behind closed doors. The prosecutor was arguing his side to present a final witness. Mr. Emerson was willing to listen to the prosecutor's argument even though this witness in question was not listed as one of the people scheduled to testify. The judge, too, was willing to give the prosecutor time to state his case even though he despised starting the court proceedings in an untimely fashion.

"Your honor, please bear with me as I explain my reasons for presenting a fifth witness."

Judge Anderson was putting his long black robe on as he said, "Go ahead. I am allowing you some time to do so even though it will delay today's court proceedings."

"I feel it is necessary to call my fifth and final witness. He is pertinent to this case and I realize this witness was not on my submitted list of possible witnesses."

"Well, let me hear more before I decide."

"Your honor, my witness is a person who saw the argument between Johnathan Smithson and Paul Pipford. He can attest to some of the threats Mr.Pipford made. I am able to then tie this to the case."

"Sir, with all due respect, and Mr. Emerson, I do not want what I am about to say, to be repeated to anyone."

Sidney Emerson kept silent and simply nodded his head. The prosecutor was intelligent enough to know what Judge Anderson was about to express.

"I am concerned your case at this point is weak. Unless your final witness has some rather substantial, I am fearful your case will not result in any type of a situation for the jury to render a guilty verdict."

"I understand your honor. But this witness will validate my case."

"Mr. Emerson do you have any questions or concerns?" asked the judge.

"No your honor as I reserve the opportunity to cross examine."

"Okay, I approve your final witness."

The prosecutor and Mr. Emerson proceeded to go back into the court room. The judge did likewise once the court clerk announced the judge's entrance.

PROSECUTION WITNESS #5

The prosecutor announced his fifth and final witness.

"Your honor, the prosecution now calls Ronald Rigby to the witness stand."

A man of about the age of thirty years of age entered the courtroom. He was well dressed and had a smile on his face as he seated himself on the witness stand.

The prosecutor began by saying, "Please state your name to the court."

"My name is Rodney Rigby."

"Could you tell the court your occupation?"

"I am a part time college student and I am an assistant manager at the sporting goods store in Lake Placid."

"Mr. Rigby, are you a hiker?"

"Yes sir."

"Have you ever hiked Wright Peak?"

"Yes."

"When?"

"This past Labor Day Weekend."

"Who were you with?"

"I hiked Wright Peak with my girlfriend, her sister and my brother."

"Do you know the defendant, Paul Pipford?"

"I met him atop of Wright Peak that Labor Day weekend."

"How did you meet him?"

"He was talking rather sternly to a young couple."

"Are you referring to Margaret and Jonathan Smithson?"

"Objection," stated Sydney Emerson.

The judge asked the prosecutor to not to lead the witness but he did not sustain Emerson's objection.

"How do you know the names of the couple?"

"To be honest with you, I found out their names while reading about their murders in the newspaper."

"So what was said by Mr. Pipford to the Smithsons?"

"He told them they needed to leave with him right now."

"How did they react?"

"Mr. Smithson told Mr. Pipford they were not ready to depart the summit."

"How did Mr. Pipford respond?"

"He began to get agitated and started to raise his voice."

"What did he do?"

"He approached both of them and almost came to blows with the man."

"Did you see any type of physical confrontation?"

"Well, Mr. Pipforddid place his hand on Mr. Smithson's arm as if he was going to pull him toward him but Mr. Smithson brushed his hand away."

"Did anything else occur?"

"No. Not really. Well, I mean Pipford became extremely agitated and swung his hands at Smithson but then he walked away."

"Did you see anything else?"

"No. I began to walk back over to my group. But I did hear someone fall down but when I looked over neither Mr. Pipford nor the Smithsons were in view."

"Did you go back over to the area where they were standing?"

"Yes."

"Did you see anything?"

"Yes. There was some blood on the rocks."

"Your honor, I have no further questions."

The judge said, "Mr. Rigby please wait a moment before you step down from the witness stand as Mr. Emerson may have some questions for you.

"Mr. Emerson, do you wish to cross examine Mr. Rigby?"

"Yes, your honor."

"Before you do so I would like us to take a fifteen minute break."

No one really knew why a break was being taken but the lawyers respected the judge's decision to do so.

CROSS EXAMINATION: WITNESS #5

"Well, Mr. Rigby, I am not going to take up too much of your time. But I do have a few questions."

"Okay."

"Did you witness Mr. Pipford striking anyone?"

"No sir."

"Did you intervene when Mr.Pipford allegedly yelled at the Smithsons?"

"No sir."

"When you went back to the location where the Smithsons and Mr. Pipford were arguing did you see blood on the rocks?"

"Yes sir."

"Were the Smithsons or Mr. Pipford still there?"

"No sir."

"Did you see any of them afterwards?"

"Yes."

"Who?"

"Mr. Pipford. He was descending the trail a few minutes after I saw him."

"Did you speak to him?"

"No sir."

"Did you speak to Mr. Pipford anytime after that confrontation?"

"No sir."

"So let me clarify for a moment. Did you observe Mr. Pipford strike either Margaret Smithson or Jonathan Smithson?"

"No sir."

"Your honor I have no further questions." Emerson barely finished his sentence before the judge started to ask Mr. Emerson if he was ready to present the defense witnesses.

"Yes, your honor, we are prepared to present."

"Mr. Emerson, please proceed."

"Your honor, may I ask for a bench conference?"

"Yes, Mr. Emerson. I ask for both the defense and prosecution lawyers to come forward."

The lawyers proceeded to the front of Judge Anderson's desk. The judge was curious as to what Mr. Emerson wanted to discuss, but he did have an inclination.

"Okay, Mr. Emerson, what is your request?"

"Your honor I am asking for a mistrial."

"What?!" exclaimed the prosecutor.

Judge Anderson said, "Let's meet in my chambers."

The three men settled in the judge's chambers. He then asked Mr. Emerson to explain his reasons for a mistrial.

"Clearly, your honor, the prosecution has presented absolutely no testimony or evidence for that matter to even remotely tie these ridiculous charges to my client."

"Mr. Emerson I feel you need to go back into the courtroom and present your defense. It is not my place to decide on the case. The jury has a responsibility and obligation to make a decision. In addition, Mr. Emerson, it would be highly insulting if the jury did not have that opportunity. Do I make myself clear?"

"Yes, your honor."

Once again the three of them proceeded to the courtroom to continue the trial.

THE DEFENSE

Judge Anderson settled into his seat, turned his attention to the jury, instructed them to the next step in the trial and asked Mr. Emerson to present the defense witnesses.

Mr. Emerson stood up and walked over to the jury then turned his back on the jury members and looked at Judge Anderson.

"Your honor, I would like to call only one witness to the stand. I call my client, Paul Pipford to the stand."

The judge looked baffled especially after the discussion that had ensued in his chambers. It was highly unusual for a defense lawyer to call forward his own client to testify on his own behalf, especially with murder charges.

Paul Pipford was not the least bit taken back by Mr. Emerson's strategy. Pipford proceeded to the witness stand, took the oath and sat down ready to respond to his lawyer's inquiries.

PAUL PIPFORD'S TESTIMONY

"Mr. Pipford, as the court knows, you have been charged with two counts of murder. Did you murder the Smithsons?"

"No, sir."

"Could you tell the court your occupation?"

"I own, or owned, the hiking shop in Keene Valley. I am a professional hiker and explorer."

"Did you take a group on a hike to the summit of Wright Peak this past Labor Day Weekend?"

"Yes, sir"

"How many people were on the hike?"

"Nine."

"And would you make the number ten?"

"Yes, sir."

"Did all members of your party ascend the trail together?"

"Yes, sir."

"Did every one reach the summit of Wright Peak?"

"Yes, sir."

"Did anything peculiar occur at the summit with any members of your group?"

"Yes, sir."

"Could you explain to the court what happened?"

"Each of the nine members were sitting atop the summit, eating lunch. They were enjoying the view of the mountains as I identified the various High Peaks they could see from the summit."

"Were there any concerns of yours with the group at this time?"

"No, sir."

"When lunch was over what did the group proceed to do?"

"I asked everyone to get ready to descend the mountain. At first, the group members did so but one of the people looked ill."

"Who was this person?"

"Margaret Smithson."

"Did you inquire as to what was wrong with her?"

"Yes, I asked her husband, Jonathan Smithson."

"What did he tell you?"

"He informed me that his wife had a stomach ache."

"Did you ask him anything else?"

"Yes, I asked him if his wife had been drinking any water from the stream along part of the trail."

"What did Mr. Smithson tell you?"

"He said both of them had done so and he also felt rather queasy."

"What did you do then?"

"I asked them to gather their gear and proceed to descend the mountain."

"Did they do so?"

"No."

"What did they do?"

"Mr. Smithson began to argue with me."

"Did you make any physical contact with Mr. Smithson?"

"Yes. I grabbed on to his arm as he looked as if he was going to pass out."

"How did he react?"

"He pushed my hand away."

"Did you raise your voice?"

"Yes, somewhat. I insisted they come down the trail with the group."

"Did you depart the summit with the group?"

"No, not at first. I sent the rest of the group on ahead as I tried to persuade Mr. and Mrs. Smithson to come with me."

"What did they do?"

"They sat down by the crevice of the summit and did not come with me when I began the descent from the peak."

"When you completed with the hike, did you ever see the Smithsons again?"

"No. I assumed they eventually made their way down from the summit."

"Did anyone ever notify you that they were missing?"

"No, sir."

“Did anyone ever question you, prior to your arrest, about the Smithson’s hike to the summit of Wright Peak?”

“No, sir.”

“Again, Mr. Pipford, I am asking, did you murder Margaret and Jonathan Smithson?”

“No, sir, I did not.”

“Your honor, I have no further questions for my client.”

Judge Anderson waited for Mr. Emerson to return to his seat. Then the judge stated he wanted a fifteen minute recess after the prosecutor said he would like to cross examine Paul Pipford.

CROSS EXAMINATION OF PAUL PIPFORD

The trial proceedings were convened exactly fifteen minutes later. Judge Anderson asked the prosecutor to proceed with his cross examination of Paul Pipford.

"Mr. Pipford, are you an experienced hiker?"

"Objection. Your honor, this has already been well established. We do not need to waste the time going back over Mr. Pipford's credentials. We all know he has hiked all forty six of the High Peaks along with numerous other trails."

"Sustained," the judge somewhat murmured. "Please get on with it sir."

"Mr. Pipford, do you often take groups up to the summit of Wright Peak?"

"Yes."

"Are you familiar with the history of the airplane crash that occurred atop Wright Peak?"

"Yes."

"Do you educate your hikers of the tragedy?"

"Yes."

"Were the Smithsons curious about the details of the crash?"

"I guess so."

"You guess?"

"Well, I do not really know how curious they were about it."

“Are you familiar with the crevice where pieces of the aircraft are still visible?”

“Yes.”

“Did you know the bodies of Margaret and Jonathan Smithson were discovered there days after your hiking excursion?”

“Yes.”

“Mr. Pipford, why did you allow the Smithsons to drink tainted water from the stream?”

“I did not allow them to do so. I did not know about that until after I questioned why they both felt ill.”

“Did you place your hand on Mr. Smithson and knock him to the ground?”

Yes. I did so because he looked as though he was going to pass out.”

“What did Mr. Smithson do?”

“He pushed my hand away.”

“Did you raise your voice to the Smithsons?”

“I raised my voice and insisted they return with me.”

“Why didn’t you stay with the Smithsons when they took ill on top of Wright Peak?”

“They did not want me to stay nor did they want my assistance.”

“Did you not feel they were your responsibility?”

“No. Each hiker signs a contract. One part of it states if a hiker wishes to depart from the group at any time during the hike outing, they may do so at their own risk. Thus we are not liable for any responsibility."

"Mr. Pipford, did you murder Margaret and Jonathan Smithson?"

"No, I did not."

The prosecutor reluctantly walked away from the witness stand, said out loud to the judge that he had no further questions.

CLOSING ARGUMENTS

Both Mr. Emerson and the prosecutor presented their closing arguments. Surprisingly both of them were brief. Even more so, Mr. Emerson who has a reputation for being long winded with closing arguments, spoke for even a shorter time than did the prosecutor.

Upon completion of the closing arguments, Judge Anderson instructed the jury as to their obligation to decide on the verdict of the defendant, Paul Pipford. He reiterated that Mr. Pipford has been charged with two counts of murder. He instructed the jury members that they could find the defendant guilty with no reasonable doubt.

The jury went into the jury room and began deliberation. The media and attendees in the courtroom scattered outside to await the jury's verdict.

THE JURY"S DECISION

The jury informed the court clerk, after less than ninety minutes of deliberation, that they had reached a decision.

The jury reassembled in the court room. Judge Anderson reappeared and asked the jury foreman if the jury had reached a verdict.

"Yes, your honor, we have."

"Please hand your decision to the court clerk."

The judge looked at the sheet of paper, looked up at the courtroom and then asked Mr. Pipford to rise. He did so along with his lawyer, Mr. Emerson.

The judge began to read the jury's findings,

"On the charge of murder of the first degree of Margaret Smithson we find Paul Pipford innocent."

Crying could immediately be heard from both Margaret and Jonathan Smithson's family members.

The judge continued, "On the charge of murder of the first degree of Jonathan Smithson we find Paul Pipford innocent."

"Members of the jury the court thanks you for your time. Mr. Pipford you are free to go."

****

Paul Pipford was elated. He hugged Sydney Emerson and departed the courtroom with Emerson. The media was ready to ask so many questions, but Pipford just continued to smile, got into Emerson's car and they proceeded to drive away from the chaotic scene.

Sydney Emerson had become a household name. He knew he had greatly bolstered his reputation as an astute lawyer.

PART SIX

CHAPTER FORTY

HOUGH PEAK IS RARELY CLIMBED BY HIKERS BY ITSELF…

Matthew was about to approach the house when he spotted headlights coming up the driveway. Had someone found out his whereabouts? When the car stopped he was taken back to see Rita Metcalf emerge from the vehicle. Long before Rita married Ryan, Matthew had dated Rita a few times. He figured Rita knew he was alive. And she probably already discovered he was in the area. He knew the news of his reappearance was known by many. This would include people who had not read so in the local newspaper. Since that was the case he figured he had nothing to lose by proceeding to the front porch of Anna's, and formerly his, house and confront the people inside.

The door opened up and Sean came onto the porch to retrieve a few logs for the fireplace. Even with the front light on, it was rather dark. Only a small amount of light illuminated the porch and barely shined onto the yard and snow covered driveway. Sean picked up five logs and went back into the house. Sean did not realize Matthew Hamilton was only about ten feet away from the porch.

Suddenly a gunshot was heard off in the distance. That seemed rather odd especially since it was already nightfall. The gunshot could not possibly be from a hunter. Sean reopened the front door. He had a flashlight in his right hand. He could hear some rustling in the woods but could not see anything moving. The snow was coming down lightly. Even though Sean only had a short sleeve shirt and jeans on, he looked around the house to see if anything was disturbed. He noticed some footprints but he believed they were Sabrina's and his along with his mother's. He went back inside. The snow was expected to curtail by morning.

MATTHEW HAMILTON

"All will be well…unless…"

Matthew Hamilton had lived in the Keene and Keene Valley area his whole life. He had never completed high school as he seemed to always be assisting his father with their farmland. The farm business was not a real prosperous enterprise for the Hamilton family. But when his father took ill when Matthew was in ninth grade, Matthew began to miss an enormous amount of school. The county truant officer tried to re-engage Matthew in his school studies but the necessity for Matthew to assist his father took precedence.

One thing that did distract him from his chores on the farm was his love of Rita. They were one grade apart from one another in school. He was older than her but by the time she reached the tenth grade, they were in classes together as Matthew had fallen behind in his studies.

Matthew did not marry until he met Anna. Matthew had always hoped to wed Rita but that was not to be the reality of his life. Once she met Ryan Metcalf, Matthew realized his chance of being with Rita was nil.

Matthew had known Sid Mesier for years and over time he had become acquainted with his wife Anna. Before ever meeting Anna formally he knew of her as most people in Keene knew one another. Matthew also realized Sid had invested well in land and stocks so he knew the Mesiers were well off, especially compared to most families in the area.

Matthew also knew that Anna was deeply in love with Sid. Sid often talked about Anna whenever Matthew and Anna socialized. Sid often referred to Ann as his goddess. Matthew could tell that Anna was the most important person in his life. The love Sid had for Anna was mutual. Everyone in Keene knew how much the two of them treasured one another.

With this in mind, upon Sid's untimely death, Matthew tried to woo Anna even though replacing Sid would be a monumental task. But Matthew's ulterior motive was garnering Anna's fortune. Matthew knew Sid was a rather savvy person when it came to investments.

Matthew's other so called obstacle was Anna's daughter, Sabrina. He realized Sabrina never took a liking to him but he tried to make it look to Anna as if all was well between himself and Anna's daughter. Matthew was able to persuade Anna that everything would work out between Sabrina and himself. But he knew Sabrina would never get along with him. He was always concerned that Sabrina knew what his motives and intentions were all about. Sabrina seemed to also be able to read right through Matthew. He often wondered how he could change Sabrina's perception.

CHAPTER FORTY*ONE

GIANT MOUNTAIN IS A LARGE LAND MASS TOWERING OVER KEENE VALLEY…

Matthew Hamilton stumbled down the trail when the gunshot was heard. He realized this could not be a gunshot attributed to a hunter. The gunshot had to be from a local resident scaring off a bear or perhaps coyotes. Coyotes were always a concern in this region of the Adirondacks. It has always been highly unlikely that a coyote would be visible during the day time but the chances have always been good that the coyotes could be heard during the night. Sometimes their howling would be high pitched. The coyote is a predator and people have always been concerned about their smaller pets being attacked.

Sean reopened the front door. He came out onto the porch and had a hunting rifle in his hands. As he looked around, a car came up the driveway. Sean immediately recognized it to be Sydney Emerson's vehicle. Mr. Emerson, Sean's lawyer, was in the passenger seat and his father was driving Emerson's car. Now Sean knew where his father had been. But why hadn't his mother told him that.

Sean waited on the front porch until they came out of the car and made their way to the house. Sean was still concerned with the gunshot he had heard. But that was not his main concern.

Matthew came back up the trail and peered at all of them from behind a tree. He recognized Ryan Metcalf but was unsure of who the other man could be. Suddenly he recognized the man's bulky frame and slight limp. He knew it could only be the infamous Sydney Emerson. Matthew became extremely agitated. He wanted to make his presence known but he knew this was not yet the place or time to do so. This man had altered his life dramatically. He trusted this man. Sydney Emerson had fooled so many people in believing that he was a man of principles.

This was the man who had planned Matthew's disappear

CHAPTER FORTY*TWO

THIRTY YEARS AGO

MOUNT REDFIELD WAS NAMED FOR PROFESSOR WILLIAM C. REDFIELD, METEROLOGIST, ORGANIZER OF AND PARTICIPANT IN, THE FIRST RECORDED ASCENT OF MT. MARCY…

Matthew Hamilton was attending a lawyer's convention in New York City. The weather was quite warm for a January day. The temperatures were in the sixties. And just last week there had been a major snowstorm blanketing the city with over fifteen inches in many locations. The metropolitan area had become immobilized. But now it looked as if the storm had never occurred.

Matthew Hamilton had formally met Sydney Emerson at the convention. Hamilton knew of Emerson by his reputation which had preceded him but he never crossed paths with Sydney Emerson in Keene or the surrounding area. That, in itself, seemed odd since Hamilton lived in the region all his life. Emerson's family had resided in Keene,too,for quite a few generations. During the 1930's things were particularly difficult for the family. The same was apparent for the Hamilton family. That was true for many people as the Great Depression had affected the rural areas of the United States more so than anyone thought.

Hamilton was struggling to garner clients for his law office. He had experience with elder law, will drafts and tax cases. His office consisted of himself and his secretary, his sister. He went to the New York City convention hoping to gain further employment so he could become a more prominent attorney. His law practice was not flourishing. By a bit of chance, his path crossed with Sydney Emerson.

Hamilton was taken in by Emerson's overwhelming personality and abrasiveness. Hamilton had always heard about Emerson's disposition, but since he had not met him before this time he was somewhat taken by both Emerson's physical size and overwhelming personality.

Overbearing and obnoxious, yet a successful and well-to-do lawyer, Emerson took Hamilton under his wing and assisted him with becoming a better, and somewhat cutthroat, lawyer. Hamilton, though, felt he could never come out from under Emerson's stranglehold. He feared leaving Emerson; Emerson in so many words threatened to bad mouth Hamilton if he ever departed. Naturally, Hamilton knew Emerson feared him taking away some of his clients. But Hamilton knew there had to more to it than just simply Emerson being concerned about losing clients.

Matthew's sister continually warned him about Sydney Emerson's fiendish ways. But Matthew ignored her insistence to beware of Emerson and his doings. A few short weeks after Hamilton had returned from New York City, his sister suffered a massive brain hemorrage. She died two days later. Matthew was left with the unfathomable task of taking his sister off the life support system. She expired thirty minutes after he did so. He also realized he could not continue to maintain his law office without her.

Matthew Hamilton became a protégé of Sydney Emerson. The connection between the two of them would become somewhat twisted later in life

CHAPTER FORTY*THREE

PRESENT DAY

CLIFF MOUNTAIN IS A DIFFICULT SOMEWHAT MUNDANE HIKE…

Matthew realized Anna, Sabrina, Sean and Sean's parents did not realize what Sydney Emerson had done to him. In fact, Matthew Hamilton realized it was improbable Anna and his stepdaughter, Sabrina, along with the Metcalf family would believe his story. He knew he was partially to blame for the predicament he had put himself in. He also realized he should have never gotten involved in Emerson's scheme yet he had become so consumed by gaining immediate wealth his sense of reality was distorted. He knew he was not blameless.

Matthew began to talk out loud to himself.

"I need to see Anna."

He looked over at the house he used to live in. The outside of the house had not changed since he had departed. The bushes around the house had become overgrown though. He could not tell how the lawn looked as it was covered with the snow and ice.

"Anna will be so angry with me. I need to let them know about Emerson."

He found himself talking to himself out loud. He needed to be careful or any of them could hear him. He was becoming more and more angry. Matthew knew Emerson would try to convince Anna, Sabrina, Sean and Sean's parents that he was a murderer. But Matthew knew better. His concern would be how convincing Emerson could be. Emerson had been a manipulator all his life. Matthew was surprised that Sean's father could not figure Emerson out. Ryan was a detective by trade so he should be able to look through what Emerson would tell them. So maybe he already had an inclination that Emerson was not all he made himself out to be. Matthew could only hope that would be the case.

****

Matthew decided he needed to think things out. He could not just yet proceed and knock on the door. He needed to decide upon some sort of strategy. He pondered and thought to himself as to where he could go in the meantime. Wherever he might try to find a place to stay, his picture was not only in the newspaper but also posted on the internet and exhibited in every shop in Keene and the surrounding towns. This included being so at the post office, the bank, the motel and the fire station.

Keene is a small, close knit village. Everyone was talking about his reappearance. He had to tell his story to someone. Emerson had become a formidable foe. But Hamilton realized he needed to outsmart Emerson. Perhaps he could confront him one on one. Physically Emerson is quite imposing so Hamilton understood he would need some other way to intimidate Emerson. Could he bring Police Chief Winston into the loop? Or would he need to rely on someone else?

CHAPTER FORTY*FOUR

SANTANONI PEAK IS OFTEN CLIMBED WITH PANTHER OR COUCHSACHRAGA PEAK…

Sabrina was in the kitchen with Sean. She looked quite harried. Even though she wanted to be here with her mother she felt something just wasn't right. Her intuition in the past had always been correct. She was boiling water for tea, as Sydney Emerson sat with Rita, Ryan and Anna in the living room. The room was warm as a roaring fire was ablaze in the fireplace.

At first, each of them seemed rather hesitant to begin a conversation. Emerson was still adjusting himself into a chair by the fireplace even though he seemed to be sweating. He took off his suit jacket. Rita was taken back at how heavy Emerson appeared to be. She knew he had always been a heavy individual, but his appearance somewhat concerned her, especially due to the fact that Emerson was sweating and it was the middle of the winter.

Sabrina came into the living room area with a tea kettle, teacups and saucers, sugar and milk. Sean followed behind her with a coffee cake and cookies. Anna had baked them earlier in the day as she awaited any news on the situation. She needed to keep herself busy and she usually cooked or baked whenever she was anxious or nervous. People throughout Keene were aware of how great of a baker Anna could be when she was up to the task. The local eatery owner would often ask Anna to bake her delicious blueberry and raspberry pies.

Sean's mother, Rita, got up and helped Sabrina serve the cups of tea. Emerson was still moving around in the chair. He looked quite uncomfortable. Then he spoke,

"So let's get started. We all know Matthew Hamilton is alive. We know he is in town somewhere and we know he is going to attempt to make contact with one of you."

Each of them looked at one another. Again, though, none of them spoke. They were unsure of what Emerson was going to imply. Their silence did not curtail Emerson from not only continuing the conversation but controlling it as well. And that suited him fine.

Emerson continued,

"It will probably be you, Anna, or you, Sabrina."

There was some shifting around by each of them. Emerson seemed to be talking in a mysterious manner and not with a sense of urgency.

Anna spoke up first.

"But why? And why now?"

Anna looked utterly drained by the turn of events. She got up from her chair and walked over to the living room window. Sabrina stood up as well and walked over to her mother and put her arm around her mom. She tried to comfort her mother but she was concerned as Anna was trembling.

Anna then turned to Emerson and said,

"What about the death of Sid?"

Emerson did not respond.

She hesitated and then asked another question.

"Are you implying Matthew committed the murder of Sid?"

Emerson simply stated,

"Yes. Why don't you think so?"

"What?"

Emerson pushed himself up and out of the chair. He was perspiring profusely. He took a few steps toward Anna and said,

"He did it to get to your monies!"

CHAPTER FORTY*FIVE

ALLEN MOUNTAIN IS A MAJOR UNDERTAKING AS IT IS A NEARLY TWENTY MILE ROUNDTRIP…

The judge was meeting with Police Chief Winston to regroup. The sudden change of events with the reappearance of Matthew Hamilton had drastically altered the investigation. In all his years as a law agent, Winston told the judge he had never seen such a bizarre case. The judge wholeheartedly agreed. The thing that made the case so baffling to Winston was that after all his years residing in Keene, he felt as if he had a handle of the daily activities of the people of Keene. But to witness Anna Hamilton being so distraught, he realized he needed to tap into his expert investigative skills to tackle the situation.

Winston and the judge were awaiting the arrival of Keene mayor Galente so they could update him on the quickly changing details of the case.

****

The door of the police station opened up rather abruptly and entering was Sydney Emerson. In a booming voice he said,

"Good morning gentlemen!"

The judge spoke up first.

"How are you Sydney?"

"Well, thank you. I understand all charges are dropped against my client, Sean Metcalf. Correct?"

Both the judge and the police chief hesitated to respond.

"Is it true or not?"

Emerson was becoming impatient rather quickly, even more so than his usual behavior. He was breathing heavily and his cheeks were almost crimson. He was wearing a bulky winter overcoat. He was sweating profusely.

Again there was a hesitation to respond to Emerson but then the chief nodded affirmatively. With that Emerson pressed both men for updated details.

Police Chief Winston stated,

"There is nothing to report. In fact, the case should no longer interest you unless you represent Matthew Hamilton."

Emerson raised his eyebrows and then turned his back on the judge and the police chief and walked toward the exit. As he approached the doorway, the door suddenly opened and Mayor Galente entered. The winds outside were howling and snow was coming down heavily.

Emerson walked past Mayor Galente without acknowledging him. Emerson walked to his car located across the road. He got into it and departed in a fast manner even with the roads being snow covered.

Galente, looking somewhat angered, exclaimed,

"Why was Emerson here? I have never trusted that bastard!"

SID MESIER

"There are no hopeless situations."

Sid Mesier was a hardworking man. He knew how to invest his money wisely. Even though he would take risks sometimes, they were calculated risks. His most thought out investment was a series of tracts of land in the Adirondacks region. Some of these plots of land had old time cottages built on the acreage. He hired a number of workers who were able to revitalize the cottages. Once these projects were completed he rented the cottages out for both long term and short term dwellers.

These cottages became rather profitable. Sid also invested in a few horse farms. These, as well, became profitable as Sid knew three men who were quite experienced in the field of breeding and taking care of horses. One of these men was a local friend, Matthew Hamilton. Another of his acquaintances was a man named Jason Euling. He later became a law enforcement agent.

Sid met AnnaHenery, daughter of Jane Henery, when he was sixteen years old. Upon meeting her at a church picnic, he found her to be very shy yet she had a beautiful smile and bright blue eyes that shimmered like glass when the sunlight bounced off them. Sid was always writing love letters to Anna. He had an incredible talent with expressing his feelings in writing. He knew Anna had kept each and every letter he had sent her. He came upon the letters tied up in red and green ribbon. The letters were in a chest stored in the attic.

Sid had called upon Anna with her father's permission the following weekend. Anna's father drove Anna and Sid to the movie house in Lake Placid. Sid could not remember what the film they went to see but he treasured their evening together. Anna's father waited for them to come out of the movie house. Anna's dad drove them to a local ice cream stand. Both Anna and Sid ordered vanilla cones with chocolate sprinkles as Anna's dad again waited for them. This time he did so by walking down to the lake and smoked a cigarette.

Anna's father drove them back to Keene. He dropped off Sid at his house which was a half a mile away from the Henery's house. About three years after dating Anna, Sid asked Anna to marry him. Naturally this was after asking Anna's parents for her hand in marriage. They got married and a little over a year after they were wed Sabrina arrived. But a week later, Anna's dad was found dead in his workshop. Apparently he had suffered a stroke. Sabrina and her mother, Anna, were devastated. He was only forty one years old.

CHAPTER FORTY*SIX

BLAKE PEAK WAS NAMED AFTER MILLS BLAKE, VERPLANK COLVIN'S ASSISTANT DURING THE GREAT SURVEY OF THE ADIRONDACK PARK…

Sydney Emerson returned to his house located on a sixty-acre farmstead. He lived alone as his wife left him years ago. They had no children together even though she wanted to have a family. He seemed to always be too consumed with his work and did not cater to his wife. Sydney was the last of his family to reside in Keene. Emerson's family had contributed so much to the community, including the pavement of the roadway to Elizabethtown. That project was quite an ordeal but the men on the job were quite determined to complete their mission.

Emerson began to pack an overnight bag and readied himself to depart within the next hour, especially since the snow was falling rather heavily. He placed two sets of underwear and socks into the bag first. Then he placed a pair of pants and a bulky sweater into the case as well. He took a small caliber gun out of his night table, placed it into a dark blue container and placed it underneath the clothing he had just placed into the overnight bag.

The sound of Emerson's cell phone startled him. It was as if someone saw him place the weapon into the case and into the overnight bag. His nerves were on edge; this was something he never really experienced before. The cell phone rang four times before he answered it.

"Hello!" Emerson was out of breath. His breathing was jagged.

At first, there was no response.

"Hello?" repeated Emerson.

"Yes. Is this Sydney Emerson?"

"Yes. Who is this?"

The cell phone went dead and an abrupt knocking occurred at the front door.

****

Emerson was sweating and he was becoming rather anxious. He slowly approached the door. The knocking occurred again. Without saying anything or even looking to see who could be knocking, Emerson opened the door.

Emerson looked startled and gasped,

“What are you doing here?”

The person at the doorway just leered at Emerson, passed by him and walked into the main room of Emerson’s house and began to laugh.

“How dare you come here!”

The person stopped laughing, but continued to smile and said,

“Don’t even take that tone with me! You know you can go to prison for the rest of your life,” said Matthew Hamilton. “And you are going to do what I tell you. You have done enough harm. I need to get my life back!”

REVEREND METCALF

"Never underestimate the power of your actions."

Things were getting complicated. As they departed the remote cabin he spotted the black SUV he was warned would be coming upon the place. Also, of utmost importance, his wife was rather suspicious of why they were suddenly departing the cabin. Things were serene all day Saturday and then the reverend insisted on their immediate departure. He felt like a captured animal. Or worse yet, he felt like a runaway convict.

The reverend had often preached to his followers to always remember that the truth would set you free. He was far from following that advice. He surely could not inform his wife that he has a whole other family living in the Adirondacks. His wife Patricia was an intelligent woman. She knew something had gone awry yet she was more frightened than anything else with her husband's sudden change of plans.

"Dear, why are we leaving so soon?"

"Please we need to leave now."

The reverend could not think of a valid reason that his wife would understand and also not question him on. He needed to stall for time. They quickly packed up their car and departed from the scenic cabin they had so been looking forward to spend the weekend. Patricia could barely collect all of their belongings as her husband, Edgar, was pacing the room in a rather rapid fashion.

"Please, honey, tell me what is going on. You seem to be spooked."

"I will tell you in the car. Let's go!"

Reverend Metcalf realized he must appear to be acting irrational but he knew if the unknown person who was going to be approaching the cabin at any moment and discovered him and his wife at this remote place, he would be doomed. He was sure that his son, Ryan Metcalf, had been keeping close tabs on him for years. Fortunately he had never gotten as close as now.

The reverend knew that his son's most recent situation involved the mind boggling arrest of Ryan's son, Sean Metcalf. Believe it or not, the reverend had tears come to his eyes as the realization that his grandson, Sean, who he had not ever met, was arrested for the murder of Matthew Hamilton. And worse yet, he knew that Sean was innocent of the charge as his contact person, Sydney Emerson, had set up a scenario to make it look as if Sean committed a murder. The reverend was amazed that Emerson could be so manipulative whereas he was defending Sean for the murder of Matthew Hamilton, he was also sabotaging the case as if Sean committed murder.

Reverend Metcalf knew he could not expose Emerson's scheme. He knew he would then reveal that he is alive. His first family would be overwhelmed. His first wife, Mary, still resided in Keene. Mary raised their two sons, Michael and Ryan, on her own. The reverend knew that she spoke little of him. This was often conveyed to Edgar Metcalf by Sydney Emerson.

But now the reverend was concerned about the person coming to the cabin to find him and his wife. He was also conflicted with what he should tell his wife, Patricia. And now the startling fact was that his grandson, Sean, was in dire straits for something he did not do.

The reverend pulled out the vehicle in erratic fashion. Patricia was extremely concerned about their safety as the road was not paved well. She asked him if he wanted her to drive instead.

"No. I can manage this!" he said in a raised voice.

During all the time they had been together, the reverend had never raised his voice to her with such anger. She was becoming shaken by his behavior. As they turned out of the driveway, he sped quickly down the road looking constantly in the rear view mirror and side mirrors. Patricia knew something was amiss. Just then the reverend's cell phone began to ring. He answered it on the third ring.

"Yes!"

"He is approaching the cabin now. Where are you?"

"We have left already. We are on our way back to our house."

"What did you tell your wife?"

"Don't worry. We are fine."

With that the reverend disconnected the call. All Patricia could do was look at her husband.

He simply said, "There's been an emergency. We need to go home."

Before Patricia could respond he said,

"And our daughters are fine. There is nothing to concern yourself with."

Patricia just closed her eyes and silently prayed. Edgar realized he would have to give his wife an explanation about the abrupt departure. He dreaded the possibility of telling her a fabricated story. But he knew he may not have an alternative as their lives could get extremely complicated. He was totally torn over what to do. His son, Ryan, always believed he was alive. And Sydney Emerson had complicated so many people's lives. He wished he had never came in contact with Emerson. The reverend's life was about to be turned inside out. How could he control the spiral?

CHAPTER FORTY*SEVEN

PANTHER PEAK DOES NOT HAVE ANY PANTHERS OR MOUNTAIN LIONS ON IT…

The Metcalf family gathered at their home. Ryan's brother, Michael, had even made the trip over from Lake Placid. All of them seemed relieved that Michael was with them as well. Ryan had always looked up to Michael. This had always been so ever since their father, Sean's grandfather, had mysteriously disappeared so many years ago. Sean, to this day, always wondered if his grandfather was still alive somewhere.

Sean was happy he was free of any pending charges. But, yet, he was extremely concerned about Sabrina and her mom, Anna. Sabrina was with Anna at the police station. Police Chief Winston sat with Sabrina and Anna at his office.

Police Chief Winston began by saying,

"Mrs. Hamilton, we are not sure where Matthew is at this time."

He looked at both Anna and Sabrina before he continued.

"He was spotted, though, outside your house earlier today."

Sabrina spoke up.

"By whom?"

"Sean."

Sabrina turned to her mother and said,

"What? Why didn't he say something? Wait. Sabrina, you knew too?"

Anna got up from her chair. Sabrina looked exhausted; she began to cry. But Anna was not sympathetic at this time. She directed her comments to Sabrina but did not look in her direction.

"Sabrina, do not keep anything from me! Especially with everything that has happened! You mustn't keep anything from me. I am frightened for both of us. And you have a baby to worry about!"

Anna then turned to Sabrina and said,

"I need you more than ever. Matthew is not your father."

"I know that."

"And I am afraid he may have murdered your Dad."

Sid Messier, Anna's first husband, had been found in the woods. A gunshot was discovered in his skull. Anna never really believed Sid Messier had committed suicide as she was led to believe. She regretted not having the local authorities complete an autopsy as they had so strongly suggested. She was too upset at the time to think logically. If only her father had been alive at the time he could have reasoned with her. Her mother did not have that ability to do so.

****

The police chief had listened intently to Sabrina and Anna's conversation. He felt he needed to provide them with some details of the police investigation. He reluctantly interrupted their conversation as he was both somewhat embarrassed by what he heard Anna and Sabrina discussing and he knew he was responsible for informing them of the status of the case.

"I need to tell both of you that we are concerned about your welfares. I do not want you to return to your home tonight. We will place you at a hotel in Lake Placid. I have already booked two rooms at the Crowne Hotel. The one room will be for the both of you. The second room is for a law enforcement agent I have been utilizing during the investigation of the case."

"Why? What do you need to tell us about?" Anna inquired.

Anna seemed somewhat calm, but more than likely it was because she was fatigued. Sabrina held hands with her mom as the police chief went forth with an explanation.

"We believe Matthew faked his death so no one could pick up any leads."

Neither Sabrina nor Anna looked surprised.

"But we also feel he had an accomplice to orchestrate his faked death."

"What?!"

"I believe someone local was paid by Matthew to set up this entire scheme."

Both Anna and Sabrina looked baffled.

"Who?" they said simultaneously.

The police chief hesitated. A car approached the police station. A man got out of the vehicle holding a baby and made his way into the station. Sabrina went to the police office entrance. It was Sean and he was carrying their baby. Sean and Sabrina hugged one another with the baby between them. The baby began to cry. Sabrina placed the baby into her arms and rocked him back and forth as the three of them went into the police chief's office.

CHAPTER FORTY*EIGHT

THE FULLTIME POPULATION OF ADIRONDACK PARK IS JUST OVER 100,000…

Emerson attempted to depart his house but Matthew Hamilton would see nothing of it. Hamilton realized Emerson outweighed him by at least one hundred pounds. He knew he had to deter Emerson from departing. Hamilton was somewhat concerned that Emerson would push him aside but he knew he needed to show Emerson he was in charge.

"Do you really think you are going to leave and desert me? I think not. Now sit down!"

Emerson ignored him and proceeded to pick up his overnight bag and moved toward the front door.

"Emerson, do not open that door." Hamilton said calmly.

"Or what?"

Hamilton fired a shot into the ceiling. Emerson jumped, turned around and stared at Hamilton. Emerson never expected Hamilton to utilize a gun. Emerson always thought of Hamilton as being a timid individual. He had never exhibited to Emerson any real nerve with anything. And that is why Hamilton never really became any type of a good or for that matter a reliable lawyer.

"Now, sit down like I told you."

Emerson listened to Hamilton. All Hamilton did was grin and realized he had control over Emerson. He finally felt he could control the situation.

****

A set of headlights illuminated the long driveway. Emerson's sixty-acre farm was mostly over grown. The days had long past since cows grazed the land and potatoes were harvested. Emerson had always hired farmhands capable of sustaining the farm business. Surprisingly a profit was always garnered.

Hamilton peeked out the window and saw there was a police car with one officer in it. It was Sergeant Tedesco. Hamilton told Emerson to answer the door and act normal. He warned Emerson that he would have the gun pointed at Emerson. He then instructed Emerson to remain calm and see why Tedesco was here. Hamilton felt Emerson was finally listening to him. This was something Hamilton had never experienced with Emerson before. Emerson had always been a belligerent individual. He never showed any respect toward anyone and that included his clients and any lawyer he opposed. But now the tables had turned.

Tedesco rang the doorbell. Emerson hesitated to answer the door but then did so. Sergeant Tedesco was a well-built man. He looked as if he could overpower any person he came in contact with. But the people of Keene often referred to him as a gentle giant.

"Hello Mr. Emerson. May I come in?"

Emerson moved aside without saying anything and waved Tedesco inside. Tedesco walked in and turned back around to speak to Emerson.

"Mr. Emerson, I was sent by Chief Winston to talk to you about Matthew Hamilton."

Emerson calmly said, "Yes?"

Sergeant Tedesco observed how much Emerson was perspiring even though the house seemed very cold. Emerson's large bulk seemed to cause him difficulty with standing. Tedesco realized he would have to be cautious with Emerson as Emerson's disposition was often uneven.

"Sir, are you okay? You don't look too well."

"Yes," Emerson said in a curt manner. Emerson did not make any type of eye contact with Tedesco. Tedesco noticed Emerson seemed rather jittery. This was not a characteristic known to portray Emerson. Tedesco always knew Emerson to be a calm and collected person.

"Could we sit down?" asked Tedesco.

"Fine."

Even though Emerson said yes he remained standing. Tedesco sat down on the couch. He only made this gesture as he thought it would possibly initiate Emerson to sit down as well.

With that Tedesco's attention was diverted to a noise from the back of the house. Tedesco got up from the couch. Emerson looked about the room in an odd manner.

"I thought you live alone."

"I do."

"Is there someone else here?"

"No."

Tedesco walked away from the couch and began to go toward the hallway leading to the back of the house.

"I'd stop right there if I was you."

Tedesco quickly turned and saw Matthew Hamilton standing in front of him. Tedesco realized how foolish he had been to not realize he walked into a threatening situation. His hand had been on the holster of his gun on his right hip. But he hesitated to take it out and point it as Hamilton as Hamilton had already directed his own weapon at Tedesco.

CHAPTER FORTY*NINE

MORE THAN AN ESTIMATED TEN MILLION PEOPLE VISIT THE ADIRONDACK PARK EACH YEAR…

Hamilton's appearance was not really that startling. Emerson took a few steps back as Tedesco assessed the situation.

"Why are you here?" asked Tedesco.

Hamilton looked to Emerson then back to Tedesco. The silence between them seemed long even though it was just a few seconds. Hamilton stopped pointing the gun at Tedesco. He realized it would serve no purpose to harm Sergeant Tedesco. If he was going to harm anyone it would be Sydney Emerson.

"Well?"

Hamilton just simply pointed to Emerson. Tedesco realized that Hamilton was extremely agitated with Emerson. Tedesco understood what Hamilton was trying to convey without speaking. Emerson again took a few steps toward the front door.

****

Hamilton realized his so called disappearance was bizarre. Yet to Emerson the concern was more about the death of Anna Hamilton's first husband, Sid Messier. Someone had shot Messier close range in the back of his head. To this day the murder was never solved. Initially, people of Keene thought it may have been a suicide. And Tedesco was well aware of these details as Police Chief Winston had assigned Sergeant Tedesco to the case of Sid Mesier's death.

****

There was a knock at the door. Emerson's back was almost touching the front door. He jumped forward a little with the sudden knock. Hamilton noticed how jittery Emerson had become. Emerson was soaked in sweat. His face was bright red as if he had just come in from the frigid weather. Tedesco was concerned that Emerson could have a heart attack or stroke at any moment. Emerson decided to not open the door but instead called out,

"Who is it?"

"It's Anna, Sydney, please let me in. I think I know where Matthew is. I need to talk to you."

Sergeant Tedesco passed by Emerson and proceeded to open the door. But before Tedesco could do so, Emerson pushed him aside, opened the door, ran past Anna and Sean who was there as well, and got into his car.

Tedesco picked himself up off the floor with Matthew's assistance. Tedesco was somewhat surprised that he had fallen down. No one had ever done that to him before. He blamed it on his not having a good footing more than Emerson overpowering him.

Anna could hardly believe Matthew was standing inside Emerson's house. Anna caught her breath and exclaimed,

"Why are you here?"

Hamilton walked over to Anna, took her hand and simply said,

"Sydney Emerson murdered Sid. And he also planned my disappearance."

Anna could hardly grasp what Matthew had just told her. Sergeant Tedesco was using his cell phone to contact Police Chief Winston. But he could not get hold of him.

"What?!" asked Anna. "I don't understand!"

Police Chief Winston had been standing at the doorway and overhead the end of the conversation. Tedesco looked over at the police chief. Police Chief Winston made his presence known by saying, "I can explain."

CHAPTER FIFTY

THERE ARE NO CITIES WITHIN THE ADIRONDACK PARK…

Emerson slid down the hill with his car in low gear. The roads had become treacherous. Even though the temperatures were in the low twenties, Emerson was sweating profusely. His left arm began to tingle and his vision became blurred. But this did not stop him from continuing down the road. He could hardly control the vehicle.

He was blinded by high beamed headlights. A snowplow was making its way up the hill, but Emerson did not see it until it was too late. His car slammed into the right side of the plow. The car had flipped upon impact. Even though the snowplow was not travelling at an excessive speed, Emerson's vehicle was out of control. The car slid off the side of the roadway and descended into a frozen stream. The car began to smoke.

The snow plow driver exited his truck, looked over the broken guard rail, and used his cell phone to contact the emergency dispatcher. The snow plow driver thought about making his way down to the destroyed vehicle but he realized it would be too difficult to do so. And since he was by himself he could not take the chance of jeopardizing his safety as well. From the distance he could tell there was no movement within the smashed vehicle.

Emerson had been killed instantly.

PART SEVEN

JASON EULING

"Let light shine out of the darkness."

Police Chief Mark Winston first became acquainted with Jason Euling at the police academy. The two of them had finished first and second in their graduating class. The difference between the two of them after all the grades were tallied was less than a percent. Their individual classroom and physical skills were almost identical. Often they were referred to as being "The Twins."

The amazing aspect was the absolute respect they exhibited toward one another. They never showed any type of animosity with each other. This was a rarity between such competitors. Their classmates followed their leadership skills. The captain administering the police academy classes continually praised Mark Winston and Jason Euling. But this praise was not done publically. The captain made mention of this to his colleagues only.

Over the years Winston and Euling kept in contact with one another. Even though they were quite a distance from one another, they consulted with on various cases they each encountered. Euling had been stationed in Plattsburgh for the past two years. And just three months ago Euling had asked for Winston's guidance. A rather bizarre double murder had taken place. A minister had been suspected of killing his wife and fourteen year old daughter. The twist in the case was that the minister had not been in the area when the murders took place. Yet all the evidence pointed to the minister including his fingerprints on the murder weapon. Winston was able to prove that a different caliber weapon was utilized than the one initially identified at the murder scene. The weapon used to commit the murders was registered to the minister's brother. After an autopsy was recommended by Winston, the coroner discovered a thirty eight caliber bullet instead of a twenty two caliber fired bullet. Euling was extremely appreciative of Winston's input.

So when Police Chief Winston asked for Jason Euling'sexpertise with the Matthew Hamilton case, Euling took on the role of a law enforcement agent and got an inside track on Emerson. Euling strongly recommended to Winston to carefully track Emerson as Emerson seemed somewhat slippery and elusive to Euling. Euling told Winston that Emerson could not be trusted. Euling was so right about Emerson. Winston needed Euling's perspective as a third party. Euling's insight was refreshing and it turned the case so Winston could track Emerson and discover that he had manipulated Matthew Hamilton and was scheming to garner Anna Hamilton's wealth.

But now Jason was determined to help out Ryan and his family. Ryan knew if anyone could find his father who suddenly vanished without a trace when Ryan was five years old, the person would be Jason Euling. Most recently Euling had followed well confirmed leads as to the whereabouts of Reverend Edgar Metcalf. The reverend had been most elusive as he was able to conceal himself quite well. The latest trip Euling engaged in was up to Canada to a rather remote rural area. Euling was confident he could finally find Ryan's father and confront him with his rather mysterious and baffling disappearance.

As Ryan knows, Jason's greatest attribute is to never give up on a situation, especially one that would bring such comfort to the Metcalf family if he could ever resolve the mystery.

CHAPTER FIFTY*ONE

THE ADIRONDACK PARK IS LARGER THAN ALL OF THE SEVEN SMALLEST STATES IN THE UNITED STATES: HAWAII, CONNECTICUT, NEW HAMPSHIRE, MASSACHUSETTS, DELAWARE, RHODE ISLAND AND NEW JERSEY…

Sydney Emerson was laid to rest at the Keene Cemetery overlooking the High Peaks. His plot had already been selected by him himself. All expenses had already been paid. Emerson may have been a rather obnoxious individual but his attention to detail was absolutely incredible. Just last year he had updated his will and hired an estate planner. Many people speculated as to what Sydney Emerson had bequeathed in his will.

Only twelve people attended the graveside service. Anna Hamilton and her daughter, Sabrina, reluctantly decided to attend and that was only with Sean persuading Sabrina and her mom to come with him and his parents, Rita and Ryan Metcalf.

Mayor Galente and Police Chief Winston came to the service more so to ensure calmness. The local news reporter, Wade Kapler, was on the scene too. Uncharacteristically, Kapler remained subdued and kept his distance from the gathering. Alongside him, though, was the Keene historian, Madison Schultz. Oddly, he took photos of the graveside ceremony. The local minister began to recite prayers as the attendees bowed their heads, but not really in respect of Sydney Emerson. Sergeant Tedesco attended as well. He still had not overcome his anger toward the deceased. Tedesco was annoyed that Emerson had fooled so many people and had caused so much turmoil.

Off in the distance was the twelfth person to appear at the somber event. Matthew Hamilton got into his car as the service concluded. He drove onto the main highway and departed Keene. He was never seen or heard from again by Anna or anyone else for that matter.

There was a thirteenth person though who decided to watch the burial take place. After the conclusion of the ceremony, Police Chief Winston walked over to the man off in the distance. Winston asked Sean Metcalf to walk with him.

When they had gotten to the area where the man was standing, Sean became somewhat agitated. Winston recognized Sean's apprehension. The police chief then said,

"Sean, I want you to meet a close friend of mine. I know you came in contact with him the other day. I am sorry if he acted so mysteriously."

"Hello. I am Jason Euling. And I apologize for not identifying myself to you."

Sean looked somewhat baffled until the police chief helped out the situation with a more thorough explanation.

"I asked for Jason's assistance as he is a law investigator. He specializes in murder cases, especially ones that have odd twists. He was able to quickly discover Sydney Emerson's wrongdoings. This included how Emerson was trying to set you up as the murderer of Matthew Hamilton."

With that Sean walked back over to his parents and Sabrina. They were waiting for him as Anna Hamilton had just finished speaking to Mayor Galente. The mayor was asking Anna if she could prepare the wedding cake for his daughter's wedding.

****

A few years later while visiting a friend in the Troy area of upstate New York, Sabrina picked up a copy of The Albany Post that was on the dining room table. She glimpsed at an article that read as follows:

A man, Matthew Hamilton, had been found in a submerged car in a lake by the local mall. Foul play has not been suspected as the car was driven off a boating dock. There were no skid marks. An autopsy has been performed by the Albany county coroner's office. They surmised Hamilton had suffered a massive heart attack. Next of kin was notified but no one yet has come to claim the body.

When Sabrina returned home the next day she asked her mother about Matthew's death.

Anna explained,

"I buried him once before. I could not do it again."

Sabrina just nodded her head with an understanding of how her mother felt. She had endured quite a grueling ordeal when it was discovered Matthew Hamilton was alive. Sabrina knew her mother had gone through quite a lot, especially during the last few years of her life. Her mother had once commented,

"Sabrina, my dear, please understand I feel like I have been on a never ending roller coaster ride…"

Sabrina looked over at her son, Ryan, kissed him on the forehead, picked him up, hugged him and kissed her mother goodbye. She departed from the house. Sabrina got into her car with Ryan and drove to her cabin located on top of Hurricane Mountain. She was greeted by her husband, Sean Metcalf.

Sean greeted Sabrina and his son, Ryan, at the cabin porch. The three of them went inside and turned out the lights. The snow began to fall lightly and by day break eight inches of newly fallen snow was on the ground.

Peace had been found.

EPILOGUE

"Patience and perseverance"

The Adirondacks can be both a place of beauty but also a place of mystery. Over time people have raved about the many trails, mountains, lakes and seasons of the region. But as years have passed and years go forward there will always be mysterious situations that will crop up along the way.

Sydney Emerson may have been a prominent lawyer with rather incredible legal skills, but he had also manipulated many people and the system itself. After he came to prominence with the infamous Paul Pipford case, residents had so entrusted Emerson. In their eyes, he could do no wrong, especially if Emerson defended them in a small petty case or one of a larger substance. Judges and opposing lawyers somewhat feared Emerson.

But the end of Emerson's life took a sudden turn as he was trying to pin a murder on a young man, Sean Metcalf. Emerson believed he could gain Anna Hamilton's wealth by murdering her first husband, Sid Mesier and blackmailing her second husband, Matthew Hamilton. Emerson went as far as far as to have Matthew Hamilton fake his own death. Hamilton was at a loss at the time because Emerson was going to reveal to Anna that Matthew had a previous marriage that was never dissolved. Emerson came across this rather accidentally while researching another case.

There will always be the concern by the Metcalf family not so much about the reclusive Matthew Hamilton but more so about the disappearance of Reverend Metcalf so many years ago. As Ryan Metcalf had done for so long, his son, Sean, was now determined to discover the details of the odd and sudden disappearance of his grandfather. Sean had truly inherited his dad's investigative nature.

********** **********

"If we have no peace, it is because we have forgotten that we belong to each other. Yesterday is gone. Tomorrow has not yet come. We have only today. Let us begin…"

(Mother Teresa)

LIST OF CHARACTERS

- Sean Metcalf
- Ryan Metcalf, Sean's Father; Detective; 52 years old
- Anna Hamilton, 56 years old
- Sid Messier, Anna's First Husband
- Reverend Edgar Metcalf, Ryan Metcalf's Father; Sean's Grandfather
- Michael Metcalf, Ryan's Brother; Sean's Uncle
- Jane Henery
- Ann Henery, Jane's Daughter
- Baby Ryan, Sabrina's Son
- Rita Metcalf, Ryan's Wife; Sean's Mother
- Sergeant Tedesco
- Matthew Hamilton, Anna's Second Husband
- Mayor Galente
- Lou, Printing Shop Owner
- Mildred, Lou's Wife
- Madison Schultz, Historian/Lawyer
- Sydney Emerson, Lawyer
- Wade Kapler, News Reporter
- Spencer Hamilton, Anna's Nephew
- Mark Winston, Keene Police Chief
- Mr. Smith, Hardware Store Owner
- Alexander Stevord, Longtime County Coroner
- James Boyler, Newly Appointed Coroner
- Selma Griffin, Coroner's Secretary
- Paul Pipford, Professional Hiker
- Margaret and Jonathan Smithson, Married Couple
- Jason Euling
- Patricia Metcalf
- Mary Metcalf

RESOURCES

- Adirondacks Hamlets in History: Keene and Keene Valley; Richard Plunz, Editor; Purple Mountain Press.
- Guide to Adirondacks Trails (High Peaks Region); Tony Goodwin, Editor; The Adirondack Mountain Club, Inc.
- Of the Summits, of the Forests: Adirondack Forty-Sixers.
- www.lifeinKeeneNY.com
- www.kvvi.net/library
- www.lake placid.com

ACKNOWLEDGEMENTS

As Anna Hamilton quoted her aunt, "Reading helps me to forget for a while." I hope as you were reading this book, you were able to escape life for a while. I could not have been able to write this book without God's guidance. "You can suffer anything…..if you believe in yourself and God."

The characters in the novel are fictional. The history woven into the plot of the novel is based on factual information.

I am indebted to my team of proofreaders and kind critics. They include quite a few. The first and second drafts were critiqued by my editing team: Cousin Mary Ellen Usher, Aunt Margaret Drohan and Mother-in-Law Ann Costello. They acted as a third party by providing ideas to enhance the plot and editing the prose. Behind the scenes encouragement came from Sister-in-Law Joanne Costello, Cousin Beth Drohan and other relatives, including my godmother, Eileen Horan.

The photograph on the front cover was collaborated on by my son, Michael Jr. and my godson, Ryan Costello. The inspiration of the photograph came from my brother-in-law, Jim Costello. My love for writing was enhanced by my sister, Donna McDine, along with various friends and colleagues. I am thankful for crossing paths with a new friend, Roger Hellman of Net Publisher.

My immediate family is so vital with encouraging me with working on and completing the manuscript. I am forever indebted to my wife, Maryann and our three children Colleen, Michael and Patrick. They have been incredible and extremely patient with me throughout this endeavor.

My parents, Lorraine and John, and my mother-in-law Ann and father-in-law John, have been so supportive with this writing experience. Their words of encouragement have been beneficial. As my dad has often expressed to me, "Stay strong. Don't give up!"

"REVIVE THE SPIRITS OF THOSE WHO SUFFER DISAPPOINTMENT, LOSS OR FAILURE…"